UNNATURAL DESIRES
THREE DARK TALES OF QUEER SUPERNATURAL LUST

CB CHELIAH

For my awesome beta reading team: Cassie Powers, Desiree Gonzalez (Pebbles), Charlotte Ross, Moonlight Vixxen, Dezirae Torres, Wallie Martinez-Vega, and Carmen. Thank you all! You rock!

CONTENT WARNINGS

The Knob Hill Summoning:

This book contains content some readers may find disturbing or offensive, including: Coercion, age gap, breeding/impregnation, dubious consent, homosexual acts, foreign object insertion, foreign object removal/surgery.

The Wolfman of Notting Hollow:

This book contains content some readers may find disturbing or offensive, including: Falling, broken bones, head wound, drug use, dubious consent, cocoa, sex with a mythical creature, wolfish penis, knotting, stalking/voyeur, grooming.

Vampire Motorcycle Ganged:

This book contains content some readers may find disturbing or offensive, including: Slapping, spitting, blood sports (sucking), dubious consent, choking, domination, submission, humiliation, degradation, biting, spanking and impact play, drug use (poppers), intimate partner violence (don't worry, revenge is sweet, and tastes kind of coppery).

This story features references to intimate partner violence (IPV) including physical and emotional abuse of a current partner (being physically hit/black eye and verbal slurs). Although the story is fictional, its themes reflect real-life experiences. If you or someone you know experiences IPV, please stay safe and (in the US) contact 1.800.799.SAFE (7233) or visit www.thehotline.org.

This story is about taking back control (and giving it to the right Dom).

THE KNOB HILL SUMMONING

A SHORT, QUEER, SUPERNATURAL ROMANCE

ONE

Dustin piloted, rather than drove, his old Chevy Cavalier along Circle Road. The steering wandered. The suspension threw him around. And the car bucked when shifted. So piloting was the only way to describe the relationship between the handsome teen and his dilapidated machine. To make matters worse, the potholed road and ruined shocks conspired to slam Dustin's head into the car's roof every few minutes.

On this particular Sunday, Dustin was on his way from one humanities tutoring gig to another. He'd come from Greg Fraser's house, the football star of Knob Hill High who'd lose his football scholarship if he didn't pass his senior final. Dustin's next gig was on the other side of town, and the peculiarity of Knob Hill's odd transportation infrastructure meant that he had to follow the aptly named Circle Road all the way around the town. There was no way through. All roads stopped at the Town Hall / library atop the hill. Not even the parking lot circled the building.

On the shoulder, he saw Mrs. Wetmore getting out of her car. He slowed and lowered the window. "Everything okay?"

She didn't answer, just smiled and waved Dustin on.

He couldn't see what the elderly woman clutched in her hand, but it looked like a ketchup bottle. Weird. But whatever. He had three more tutoring appointments to get to that day and would end up circumnavigating the road ringing the little town of Knob Hill.

A particularly large pothole rang Dustin's bell, and he forgot all about the librarian's odd appearance.

AFTER DUSTIN FINISHED his last appointment, he turned his rolling wreck toward the tumble-down house where he and his mother lived. Again, Dustin found himself on Circle Road, and again, he came across Mrs. Wetmore. As much as he wanted to get home, he was damn curious about what she was doing there.

The car bucked and almost stalled as he pulled up behind the librarian's dusty PT Cruiser.

"Dustin," Wetmore beamed, pocketing the same plastic bottle he'd seen her with earlier, "you're a thoughtful young man, but you didn't need to stop." Her wrinkled smile didn't reach her eyes. "I was just out here collecting oak galls."

"Oak galls?"

"Yes. Here, I'll show you." She led him over to some oaks that lined the road. "The Amphibolips Confluenta gall wasp lays its larvae in the bud of a leaf. The larvae suck nutrients from the tree and develop in a viscus fluid sack." She picked two greenish testicle looking orbs from the tree, then pulled the bottle from her pocket.

"What are you doing?" Dustin asked. Mrs. Wetmore had been 'slipping' since the death of her husband in the spring. Dustin spent a lot of time in the library, and he'd noticed a certain lack of presence, which, until now, he'd chalked up to mourning.

"I'm squeezing the juice out of them. I've decided to try making my own books from scratch, and so, I wanted to make my own ink too. I'm using them to make iron gall ink. It was invented in the fifth century, you know."

"Huh," Dustin said. Good for her. A hobby might be just the thing to get her mind off her late husband. She'd always been kind to Dustin, and he wanted good things for her. "Okay, cool. I'm going to get home now."

"Thanks for checking on me, Dustin." Her smile became a notch more genuine.

"Sure," he said, and got back in his car.

As he drove away, he noticed her bending over on the edge of the road. She must have dropped a gall.

The sky darkened. It was only four in the afternoon on an unseasonably hot June day. Weird.

Thunder split the sky apart.

Dustin jumped out of his skin.

Lightning flashed. Once, twice, a third time. Dustin's car stalled. All the dash lights died. Strangest of all, his cock stiffened in his pants and his balls tingled. As a man of eighteen, Dustin was used to spontaneous erections, but... never from lightning. Dustin turned the key. Nothing. His dick ached, pushing insistently on the waistband of his jeans.

"Goddamn it." He unbuckled his pants and undid the button, allowing his cock's livid plum tip to escape the waistband of his boxers.

"Having trouble?" A feminine voice said.

Dustin flinched so hard the seatbelt caught. He looked up into the face of officer Jane Hornbuckle and wanted to die.

She licked her lips.

Dustin's cheeks caught fire. He practically punched himself in the dick trying to cover himself.

The beautiful, rotund cop wasn't looking at his face. Her eyes fixed on his lap. "Can I help you with anything... anything at all?"

"N—no thanks."

"I'm here to protect and serve," she said. "Especially the second thing."

"I'm fine." Dustin turned the key again.

The car started.

Dustin swore he'd go to church.

CHAPTER

TWO

Monday morning, nervous excitement in the buzzing voices of Dustin's classmates didn't keep him from nodding off. As Mr. Fallaciter droned on about the atmospheric conditions necessary for heat lightning, Dustin's eyes drooped. Lack of sleep wasn't the only thing distracting Dustin. There was also the reason he was so tired in the first place, the prickling energy he'd felt in his bedroom last night. Today, added to the strange supernatural power that had the town in an uproar, were the two slivers of flesh below Mary-Jean Meretrix's thong where her skirt rode down. Dustin stared at the two slices of forbidden fruit. His eyes drooped to half-mast. While the monster in his pants rose to the same position, its broad serpentine head bumped insistently at the elastic pinch point of his boxers.

He shook himself. No time to get sidetracked. No time to wish he was that impossibly small scrap of fabric nuzzling up to Mary-Jean's musky temples of lust. The heat lightning and crackling St. Elmo's fire had kept him up, and, Dustin couldn't admit to anyone, strangely erect, most of the night. And he needed to know why. Moreover, he wasn't the only one who felt it.

The high school hallways were abuzz this morning with rumors of students getting lucky, getting it on, getting laid. But those were the popular kids. The beautiful kids. And while Dustin was undeniably handsome, he was far too big a nerd to run in those circles. And the nerds were telling a different story about the strange events and prickling energy. Kyle, his best friend and president of the math club had tossed around initials like CIA, NSA, DHS, and names like Secret Service, Military Intelligence, and MK Ultra.

Of course, Dustin had teased Kyle about needing a tinfoil hat, but the truth was that Kyle's scenario offered the only explanation for a whole town getting horny at the same time, and the 'atmospheric anomalies,' as Mr. Fallaciter called them.

His teacher's thin explanations about lightning and spring-time hormones didn't placate Dustin. They didn't explain anything. All they did, in fact, was put him to sleep. His head dipped.

Mary-Jean turned in her chair. The motion made her top bunch in a way that let Dustin see that no bra protected her large coffee nipples from rubbing on the inside of her shirt... and hardening.

"I'm going to put a baby in you," she said, her ruby lips thinning into a smile that revealed pointed shark's teeth.

"I..." Dustin stammered, scared and turned on at the same time. "Shouldn't that be the other way around?"

"Don't should on me," she said. "And no, you're going to carry my little alien baby, but don't worry, I'm going to fuck you nearly to death first." She licked her lips. "What do you think of that, Dustin?"

"I..."

"Dustin?"

He couldn't answer. Not enough information. His lizard brain just wanted the fucking, but—

"Dustin? I asked what you think of that?"

The alien baby thing, though. He'd need to know more about—

"Dustin!"

His eyes snapped open.

Mr. Fallaciter stared at him from the front of the room. "Am I boring you, Dustin?"

"I, uh, no, Mister Fallaciter. I'm sorry. I didn't sleep well."

"I asked," the elderly educator repeated, "if you believe the weather can affect the sex drive of a whole town?"

"Well," Dustin cleared his throat and sat up, bending the erection hidden by his desk in half inside his too-tight jeans, "there's seasonal depression. And cabin fever. So there is precedent for weather affecting people's emotional state."

"And is sex drive emotional, or is it hormonal?" Fallaciter asked.

"Well, the sun is a source of vitamin D, and, vitamin D affects serotonin levels, doesn't it?"

"And what does that have to do with sex drive?"

"I don't know," Dustin said. "But modern medicine is just beginning to understand the way hormones affect the body."

"And so, your argument is...?" Mr. Fallaciter prompted.

"That I don't know, and neither do you." Dustin tried not to smile. He hid his face by running a hand through his short brown hair.

The bell rang.

Dustin wanted to get the fuck out of there, but his dick still hadn't shrunken back to a size where he'd be comfortable standing up.

Dustin didn't want this conversation to continue. He grabbed his science book and held it in front of his crotch as he rose. But he didn't get the book there in time to avoid getting caught with a woody.

Mary-Jean had been reaching under her chair to get the notebook resting on the rack there. Her vee-neck sagged to reveal a lacy bra that hadn't been there in Dustin's imagination. The motion brought her eyes inches away from Dustin's bulge.

"Winning an argument with the teacher give you a boner?" she smiled.

"I...."

She turned away from him, straightening her legs to bend at the waist to retrieve her books instead. "Or did I do that?" The skirt seemed to have caught between Mary-Jean's cheeks, pulling the waist lower to reveal about half of the young woman's perfect ass.

"I..." Dustin tried again, clamping the book to his denim-clad boner.

Mary-Jean stood, turning back to him. "Seriously though. Do you believe what you said about the weather and hormones?"

"I'm not sure," Dustin replied. "I was just arguing."

"But, if there was a way to make it stop, do you think the sun...." she looked at her feet.

"I guess, maybe...." Dustin highly doubted it.

"Because I can't fucking take this," she said, meeting his eyes again. "I'm so fucking horny I'd almost do *you*." She turned and walked away.

That did it. Dustin's dick shrank to 'getting out of a cold pool' size.

THREE

Dustin lay trying for sleep, but the crack of lightning and the strange buzzing energy in his attic room kept him awake. Goddamn this heat! And these fucking tight boxers. To be fair, the boxers were only tight because he was thinking about Mary-Jean's perfect skin sliding along his own. And —

The boxers made his dick bend painfully. Dustin lifted the waistband, allowing the tip to poke out the top and point menacingly at the catch basin of his bellybutton. It didn't help. In fact, the waistband applied delicious pressure. He stretched, and the elastic pulled his foreskin back.

Fuck it. Maybe a little self-love would help him sleep. He didn't want to be a zombie at school tomorrow. The boxers slid reluctantly down his sweat-slick muscled thighs. The exposed skin prickled with evaporation, cooling Dustin slightly. He used the shorts to wipe the perspiration from his face, pausing only a moment to appreciate his own clean, musky scent as they passed his nose. He slid the bunched boxers to dry the moisture on his smooth, defined pecs. The pointed dimes of his nipples placed pleasure calls to his brain as the cloth passed.

Dustin tossed the shorts into the pile of dirty laundry hiding his hamper.

A flash of light filled the room. Heat lightning probably. Maybe a cooling rain would come lull him to sleep.

Just as he brought his hand down to start taking care of business, a chill stole over him, raising gooseflesh and sending the twin eggs between his legs diving for cover in the scant nest of blond hair.

Strange, the wispy white sheers standing sentinel on either side of the dormer window hadn't moved. The cold gray light of the rising moon played among the shadows above Dustin's bed. Frogs and crickets raised a chorus outside, and the creaky old house added to the Appalachian night song. Not a breath of air stirred to offer an explanation for the sudden cold that descended on the room.

Dustin's short hairs stood on end as an unseen energy crackled over his skin. Instead of frightening him, it aroused Dustin further. He grunted and dropped a hand down, tracing his length with the tips of his fingers. Goddamn. His lids closed, making a mental movie screen for the fantasy spectacle of tomorrow's fun.

Mary-Jean's fingers ran through his hair. The bed creaked under her weight as she sat beside him, tracing the line of his jaw with her fingers, then running along the soft rim of his ear.

"Mmmm," he moaned into the empty attic.

"Shhhh," she whispered.

Something bumped Dustin's lip. He opened his mouth and found it full of soft flesh tipped by a hard nipple. Closing his lips around her breast, Dustin sucked instinctively. The motion brought strange, sweet nectar flowing into his mouth.

Dustin's eyes flew open. This wasn't a fantasy. The breast and the mysterious fluid were real!

"Shhhh," the apparition said. She glowed a faint, rippling

electric blue against the night, sitting beside him on the bed. Her colonial era bodice pulled to the side, allowing her generous breast to meet his mouth.

Dustin tried to get up, but her impossibly strong hand pressed down on the center of his chest. When he tried to turn his head away from her breast, she palmed it like a basketball. "Suck," she said. "Drink up, you'll feel better."

Dustin nodded and swallowed the milky fluid.

"Good boy," the ghost woman cooed. "More."

Dustin's body responded to the spirit's words. His cock grew harder. A telltale drop of arousal dripped from his tip and headed down his faint happy trail.

"There you go," she said, dropping her death-grip on his skull and returning to caressing his face. "It's good, isn't it?"

Again, Dustin nodded.

The milky nectar filled his mouth. The reptile part of his brain swallowed eagerly.

"That's it," she cooed, "good boy."

Her words made him twitch, pulsing on his belly.

"Is it working?" a man's voice.

What the fuck?

"Be patient," the female apparition said.

Her hand came to rest on Dustin's, the one he'd brought down to relieve his itch. Cool, gentle, fingertips touched the soft skin stretched tight over his hardness.

"Stroke," she said. "Slowly."

Dustin's hand followed her instructions with no input from him.

"It's working," she said. "We can begin."

Begin. *Begin?* Begin what?

The ghost woman rose, her breast coming away from Dustin's mouth with a slight pop. His heart pounded against the wall of his chest.

"He looks scared," the man's voice again.

"Are you scared?" the ghost woman asked.

Dustin nodded.

"Do you want us to stop?"

His dick pulsed in his hand. It was just a dream anyway. He shook his head.

A wiry athletic-looking ghost man shrugged out of a lace-up shirt at the foot of Dustin's bed.

The female ghost bent down to him again. Crow's feet crinkled at the edge of her ghostly eyes as she smiled and took his chin in her hand. "Relax. You'll enjoy this as much as we do."

Dustin relaxed as commanded. His hand slid back and forth on his cock, coaxing another drop of one hundred proof joy onto his flat tummy.

Above him, the woman slid out of her dress, revealing the Romanesque curves underneath.

Dustin willed his hand faster, but it refused, instead continuing the painfully slow pace the apparition ordered. Goddamn.

Hands on Dustin's ankles drew his gaze down.

The male ghost spread Dustin's legs and climbed onto the bed, kneeling between them. The poltergeist's penis stood straight out, long, thick, and hungry.

Totally a dream. Hadn't Dustin had this exact fantasy? Being taken by another guy? If it was a ghost, then it wasn't gay, right? Not as gay as stealing his mother's dildo and-

The woman straddled his shoulders, blocking his view. Her sweet, earthy scent filled Dustin's consciousness. With her sex only inches from Dustin's face, she stopped, and tilted his chin to meet her eyes.

Below, the man bent Dustin's legs up and began rubbing himself back and forth along Dustin's crack, coating him with slick ectoplasmic arousal.

Dustin moaned.

"Do you want to?" the woman asked, swaying her hips, bringing herself ever closer to Dustin's hungry mouth.

Did he want to?

"Say yes, and your most intimate desires will come true tonight," the woman said, her voice soft and loving. "Say no, and we'll be gone. You can graduate Saturday, maybe knock up Mary-Jean. Live in this shitty town for the rest of your life."

"What?" Dustin whispered. Confused.

The ghost woman licked her lips, then smiled down at him. "Say yes tonight, and your life will change forever. You'll uncover the mysteries of the universe and go places you never dreamed."

The mysteries of the universe? He just wanted to cum.

"Oh," the ghost woman smiled. "you'll cum."

"Yes," Dustin said.

"Not good enough," the woman said. "Say it. Say it all."

"Please," Dustin begged, unable to think of anything but the pressure in his balls, "please fuck me and make me cum."

"Good boy," she said, then lowered herself onto his face.

The hot wet petals of her flower parted for his tongue, and he lapped their deliciousness. He groaned into her as the other ghost speared his spirithood inside Dustin's tight, but oh so willing, ass. The ghost cock bumped his prostate, sending a spasm up Dustin's spine.

"Drop your hand," the woman atop him grunted. "Don't want you finishing before I even get started." She grabbed a handful of Dustin's sandy hair and shoved his mouth harder against her sex. "Come on, suck like you mean it."

He *did* mean it. So, he sucked harder, as if he were trying to physically draw the pleasure from somewhere inside her.

The man grabbed Dustin's hips, lifting them off the bed, pushing further inside with each thrust.

Dustin's lonely cock slapped his belly to the rhythm of the man's driving need. Pre-cum dripped into his bellybutton.

"Suck, suck, suck," the woman chanted. Her fingers bumped against Dustin's nose as she mashed them back and forth across the top of her sex. She bucked her hips, alternately pushing down hard and releasing. "Yes, oooooh yes," she moaned, "it's coming."

It's coming, Dustin noted, not, *I'm* coming. The small part of his conscious mind turned that morsel of information over even as his lizard brain begged for release.

The woman smashed Dustin's head into the sheets as she bared down on him, grunting, "ugh, ugh, ugh, almost there."

Something hard inside the woman's sex met Dustin's probing tongue. He tried to speak, to let the ghost woman know.

She pulled his hair. "Don't talk with your mouth full." She pulled again. "Take it. Oh, god take it."

The hard thing inside the woman slid into Dustin's mouth. He tried turning his head to the side, but the ghost woman held his hair like a leash.

"Swallow my seed," she said.

Only in Dustin's mouth, it didn't feel like a seed at all. It felt like a pretty fair-sized egg. Dustin swallowed the hard thing, and felt it slowly working its way down his throat, loosening him up.

The spots on the edges of Dustin's vision vanished after he'd gulped in a couple breaths of air. The pale ghostly breasts above him swayed gently as the spirit rode his face to the finish.

"Ugh," she moaned. "Good boy. Now, give me that dick while he fertilizes the egg."

"WHA—" was all Dustin could get out of his mouth before the ghost cock went in. So quick was the motion that his ass cheeks didn't slam shut until the spirit's spear filled his mouth.

And then, the sensation of the woman sliding down his chest and then down his shaft.

Dustin looked up at the strong, muscled hips pumping his jaw. The sparse, coarse black hair on the ghost's chest. It seemed so real. Not ghostly at all. And the cock, salty with pre-cum, tasted like real dick. Not that Dustin had ever tasted ghost cock before.

"Breed him," the woman moaned. "Fertilize our child!"

At first, Dustin thought she was talking to him. He couldn't answer with a mouth full of spiritual masculinity, and that's when the dick's owner answered.

"Yes, love, I'm going to fill him with my love for you."

"Bring our progeny!" the woman shouted, slamming herself down on Dustin's cock.

The pressure built inside Dustin. He pushed himself inside the woman, bucking his hips off the bed. With one hand, he reached for her heavy breasts, his fingers hungry. With the other, he sought out the heavy balls slapping his chin, wanting to feel the weight of the gift his throat was about to receive.

Instead, the male ghost pulled out of Dustin's mouth.

"And just what do you think you're doing?" the female ghost asked, her voice once cultured, slipped into a thick Irish brogue.

"You said I had to fertilize the egg," the man said.

"Ya," the woman took the hand she'd been using to push Dustin into the mattress, and held it in the air at her side. "You're meant to cum in his mouth. That's where I put me egg."

"Fuck that," the man said. "And just where do you think that egg is goin? I'm meant to cum in his ass. Did you not hear Crowley's words? Did you not read the ritual? It says right in the Lesser Key of Solomon—"

"Michael," she shook her head. "You're a fuckin idiot.

Would you please just shoot a load in his mouth so we can go home?"

"Fine," the male ghost huffed.

In another universe, Dustin might have cared in which of his holes the ghost planted his seed. But in this one, he just wanted to cum. The surprise conversation, and the revelation that not only did the ghosts not really know what they were doing, but that they were putting some kind of ghost egg in him, made his dick wilt a little.

Sensing this, the female ghost slid back and forth on his cock again. "Come on big boy," she whispered. "You're going to give me the best orgasm I've had in two hundred years."

Dustin had no time to unpack that statement. The huge dripping salty cock filled his mouth once again. Sliding across his tongue and lips.

The lithe spirit on his dick humped faster, sliding her softness against his renewed rigidity.

The strangeness of the situation disappeared behind the building eruption inside Dustin.

The ghost woman's thrusts on top of Dustin forced his head forward and back on the ghost cock, sliding its tender skin across his sensitive lips.

"I'm going to cum," the man announced. He pulled out, allowing Dustin a breath before that beautiful tool blasted his lips and face with sweet seed. The ghost shoved the still bursting member back down Dustin's throat, sending a geyser of spirit seed chasing the egg deep into Dustin's belly.

"Fuck yes!" the woman slammed down on Dustin's hips, her hungry sex devouring his cock, meeting his hips, and grasping for more. "Come, now!" she commanded.

It was all too much for Dustin. These dominant, horny poltergeists devoured his cock like no human ever could. He thrust against the ghostly body above him, letting go his cum with a grunt around the softening prick in his throat.

As he filled the succulent specter on his dick, the ghost withdrew from Dustin's mouth leaving a delicious trail of salty seed pooling on his tongue, his lips, and running down his chin, dripping onto the attic floor with wet splats.

The female, bounced through the rest of her orgasm, dripping her cum and Dustin's, down his balls in a wet sticky river to the crack of his ass.

"I'm... not done," the male ghost said.

Dustin found the strength to move his eyes up the man to the hardening, wet slick ghost cock looming above him.

"Good," the woman grunted. "Fill his ass. I want to watch."

"Hey...." Dustin tried to protest. Tried to interject his will on the situation, but found his mouth filled once again with the woman's sex. He tried to shake her off, unwilling to taste his own cum, but when its salty tidepool essence touched his tongue, he sucked greedily in spite of himself.

The ghost cock that had just emptied itself inside him was already knocking hard on Dustin's back door. And, between Dustin's spit and the dribbling evidence of the ghost's last orgasm, the spirit's dick didn't need to wait on the smooth velvety porch of Dustin's cheeks. He moaned into the woman's pussy as the specter pushed inside him, sliding slowly to the hilt, making each juicy inch of that interdimensional invader work deliciously on Dustin's welcoming ass.

The guy ghost moved slow. That was fine by Dustin. As much as he hated to admit it, he loved being made love to this way, penetrated, savored, invaded. The idea that he was sexy enough to make this ghost so hard and horny brought life back to Dustin's spent dick. It slid back and forth in a pool of his cum and the evidence of the woman's viscous excitement.

All these sensations, the wet dripping folds enveloping

Dustin's mouth, the amazing dick working his hole, and his cock sliding back and forth on his belly had Dustin back on the edge of the cum cliff in a few short minutes.

"Fill him!" the woman taming Dustin's tongue grunted.

"Yes," the male ghost answered, "I'm going to whitewash his insides!"

"Ugh," she grunted, and mashed her sex down on Dustin's mouth until he saw spots again.

The man slammed deep into him. The ghost cock pulsed, throbbed, and shook Dustin.

Hot jets of ghostly fertility sprayed inside Dustin, igniting his own orgasm. Without anyone touching his cock, he shot massive jets of guy goo all over his stomach to the tune of grunting ghosts.

FOUR

The next morning found Dustin sticky and confused. Once he'd peeled himself out of bed and showered, Dustin headed for the library.

His contemporaries labeled him as a nerd. "No one goes to the library," his friend Jeff had said as he lay on a creeper under his jacked-up Corvette. But the way Jeff's shirt rose up to expose his tanned six-pack abs distracted Dustin, and he made excuses and left. "Why are you pretending like the internet isn't a thing?" Jeff called after him.

Mrs. Wetmore came around the counter when Dustin entered. "I thought you'd be getting ready for the big day," she said.

"I wanted to look something up."

She wagged a finger at him. "You're a bookish one. Go out and live your life before it's too late."

"Just one lookup," Dustin said. "Then I'll go get ready."

"Well, maybe I can speed up the process for you. I know this dusty old library better than any card catalogue."

"Well...." Dustin could feel his face redden. He didn't want Mrs. Wetmore to know about all this ghost sex magic. Plus, he might not know what The Lesser Key of Solomon was, but ghosts, plus sex, plus the name Crowley.... Ozzy wrote a song about the guy. Not something he wanted to talk about with the elderly librarian.

"I like the card catalogue. It makes me feel like Arthur Conan Doyle or something. It's so arcane I feel like I should smoke a pipe." He also liked the musty smell of the old drawers and the feel of the dusty cardstock between his fingers.

The library actually held a copy of The Lesser Key of Solomon, but when Dustin tried to find it in the stacks, it wasn't there. Fuck. Red faced and ashamed, Dustin laid the card on the counter and told Mrs. Wetmore he couldn't find the book.

"Oh," she said, grasping her reading glasses from the string of pearls around her neck and peering at the card without unfolding her glasses or putting them on. "What do you want with this nonsense?"

"It's..." Dustin would have to learn how to lie at some point. How to play poker. "It's just something I heard about."

"I see," Mrs. Wetmore said. "So you thought you'd skip school and come down to the library to look it up?" She made tsking sounds. "Follow me."

Instead of heading into the stacks, Mrs. Wetmore led him to one of the study rooms.

The horizontal blinds were closed, but fluorescent light peeped through the cracks. Someone was in there.

There was an unmistakable twinkle in Mrs. Wetmore's eye as she opened the door.

Inside, a man and a woman in dark suits poured over an old, dilapidated hardcover. Notebooks filled the rest of the table. Their open pages sported pencil drawings of strange symbols.

"Mrs. Wetmore, I asked you to see that we're not disturbed," the man said, without looking up.

"Agent Cox," Mrs. Wetmore began in a scolding tone. "This is the Knob Hill South Carolina library, not some hot shot Washington office. Besides, you told me to bring anyone who asked for that book."

The man looked up. His dark, delicious eyes met Dustin's. His heavily stubbled face showed a faint trace of a smile.

"This is Dustin," Mrs. Wetmore said. "He came in wanting to borrow a copy."

"Come in, kid," Cox said.

Dustin entered the small room. It held the over modulated scents of Old Spice and breath mints.

The handsome guy held out his hand. "Special Agent Cox, Secret Service.

Dustin shook it. "Dustin Scopae."

"We know," Cox said.

"Really?" Dustin asked.

The man smiled. He waved a hand at a pretty woman in a dark navy skirt suit who sat pouring over the book on the table. "This is Special Agent Vasinane."

The woman didn't look up, just waved a hand and kept reading.

"So," Cox said, gesturing for Dustin to take a seat, "what brings you down to the library looking for the works of Mister Crowley?"

Dustin wished they'd turn down the air conditioning. His face burned. "No reason." Stupid. He was a stupid, stupid, person.

Cox shook his head. "Tsk, tsk, tsk. You can do better."

"I—"

"Do you know what the penalty is for lying to a federal agent?"

Dustin had no idea. He shrugged.

"Nor do you want to. So, let's try again. Why did you skip

school and come down here to check out an occult grimoire of dubious quality like The Lesser Key of Solomon?"

Dustin had few memories of his misanthropic father. But he clearly remembered the thin drunken man wagging a crooked finger at him and saying, "the easiest lies to swallow come in a chocolate coating of the truth." Dustin looked the agent in the eye. "I heard someone talking about it." He didn't feel the need to mention it was a dead someone, who was fucking him at the time.

"When?" Cox asked.

"Last night," Dustin said, then winced inwardly. Now the guy would ask where. And then he'd have to make up a complete bullshit lie.

"Where?" Cox fixed Dustin with a hard stare from soft brown eyes.

Dustin's insides went liquid under the man's intense gaze. He found himself wondering what faces the agent would make if he bent Dustin over the library table... handcuffed.

"Dustin?" Cox prompted.

"What's going on in this town?" Dustin asked, pushing filthy images of Cox's hips pumping, pants around his ankles, white shirttails against hairy bronze thighs.

"What do you mean?" Cox asked.

The way he looked at Dustin. Those deep, expressive eyes. The thin traces of stubble on his chin.... Dustin could almost feel it scratching on his neck as the Special Agent devoured him. No! Stop!

"I mean, why is everyone in this town so horny all of a sudden? What's up with all the lightning at night? I mean, what's going on?"

Special Agent Vasinane looked up from the book. "When was the last time you traveled Circle Road?"

"The other day, I guess," Dustin said. "Why?"

"Which direction were you traveling?"

"To Trent's house in the East Diamond development," Dustin said.

"But which direction?"

What the fuck difference did that make? "Depends on where I'm coming from. I go both ways."

Cox raised an eyebrow.

Was the Secret Service man flirting with Dustin?

"And did you travel the entire road? Did you complete the circle?" Vasinane stared at him, her face an expressionless mask.

"I...." he'd made a bunch of stops that day. "Yeah, maybe."

"Starting in the east and traveling counterclockwise?"

Dustin rose to his feet. "Okay, what the fuck? How did you know that?"

"Someone laid out and built this whole town in the shape of a summoning circle." Vasinane tapped the cover of the book. "*This* summoning circle."

As soon as Dustin looked at the cover, a map of the town superimposed itself over the arcane symbols in his mind's eye. "Holy shit! The four big housing developments are laid out like pentagrams, with parks in the center."

Vasinane showed the first bit of personality since Dustin walked into the room. "Nice, kid. You're pretty good at this."

The dots connected slowly in Dustin's head. "And you think by driving in a circle counterclockwise I summoned something?"

Cox shrugged. "Chances of you saying the right words, having the right amulets, and thinking the correct thoughts to summon an entity from another realm are astronomical."

Special Agent Vasinane held up a finger. "But not impossible. Have you had any strange experiences? Any encounters you can't explain? Say, a situation that would make you skip school and run down to the library to get an occult book by Alister Crowley?"

The heat on Dustin's face was unbearable. He rested his forehead on the cool tabletop. "Are you armed?" He didn't care which one answered.

"Why?" Cox asked.

"Because I'd like you to shoot me," Dustin said. "It would be less embarrassing than explaining what happened."

"You had sex with a couple of ghosts," Vasinane said as if she were ordering a sandwich.

Dustin lifted his head. "How the hell did you know that?"

"Lucky guess," Vasinane said.

But, she was lying. Dustin saw the flare of her nostrils and the flush of blood in her cheeks. "You did too. That's how you know. Because it happened to you, too."

Cox looked from Dustin to Vasinane and back again. "That's uncanny. You're a natural, kid. You should come work for us!"

"Let's not get carried away," Vasinane said. "He's like twelve."

"I'm eighteen," Dustin protested. Then wished he hadn't. It made him sound immature, even in his own ears.

"Can you describe the ghosts?" Special Agent Vasinane asked.

"Bluish, solid feeling, but semitransparent. Um, a man and a woman."

"Did they speak?"

Dustin nodded, praying she wouldn't ask what they said.

"In English?"

He nodded again. Then said, "Oh, um, they had English accents until they argued, then they sounded Irish."

"Interesting," Special Agent Cox said.

Vasinane leaned in. "Did they put anything inside you? Fluids? Solids? Anything at all?"

Dustin buried his head in his hands. "Are you sure you can't just shoot me?"

"I'll take that as a yes," Vasinane said. "What substances?"

"I can't," Dustin said without looking up. He wished for death.

"It happened to me, too," Cox said, laying a warm, soft hand on Dustin's wrist.

Dustin raised his head. "Really?"

Cox nodded, his eyes soft, sympathetic, and expressive. "Really. Everything you described. A man and a woman. Both had very enjoyable sex with me. And both," he gave a sheepish smile, "made deposits in the bank of *me*. But, I can't tell you. It would contaminate our investigation. I can't lead you. You have to tell me." He glanced at Vasinane. "Tell *us*."

As Cox spoke, Dustin got that delicious pins and needles feeling under his scalp he sometimes got when he connected with another person on a deep level.

Cox nodded at him, raising his head up in invitation. Did he feel it too? That crackling energy?

And given the way the town was exploding with hormones, was this feeling of connection real, or some supernatural side effect of what had happened to Dustin the night before?

"It's okay," Vasinane prodded. "This is a safe space."

Way wrong thing to say, lady. Nothing made Dustin's asshole pucker tighter than the words 'this is a safe space.' Words that had been co-opted by parents, counselors, and school officials alike to draw secrets out of kids that would later be used to hurt them.

Cox must have sensed Dustin drawing back, because he turned to Vasinane and said, "maybe give us a minute?"

The woman frowned and pulled her blazer tighter around her full breasts. "Behave," she said, rising and leaving the room.

Dustin wasn't sure which one of them she was talking to.

The door closed.

Cox came around the table and put a comforting hand on Dustin's shoulder. It brought the bulge in the Special Agent's pants level with Dustin's hungry eyes. "It's okay, son, you can tell me."

Okay Daddy. WTF? Where did that thought come from?

Dustin tore his eyes away from Cox's crotch and looked up past the dark stubble speckling the Agent's strong jaw into his kind brown eyes. The universe swirled in his irises, the same way Dustin wanted the Treasury man's starry spend to swirl inside him.

"Dustin?" Cox whispered, his voice husky with something barely contained.

Dustin didn't break eye contact. "Yeah?"

"What did the ghosts put inside you?"

Dustin licked his lips. The erotic memories of the night before mixed with the palpable sexual energy of the moment. He dropped his eyes to the now enormous bulge in Cox's pants. The outline of the Special Agent's big dick was so pronounced that Dustin could tell the man was circumcised. He answered Cox's question in a cock-dumb trance. "Breastmilk, cum, and... some kind of egg or seed thing."

"From the female?" Cox asked.

"Yes."

Neither of them moved.

Dustin's mind clicked from thought to thought, opening dozens of evil browser tabs, searching for a way to get into Cox's pants. When he found one he liked, he threw his arms around Cox's waist and faked a sob. "It was so scary!"

Dustin rubbed his cheek back and forth against Special Agent Cox's cloth-clad shaft. "What if they come back?"

Cox moaned and dropped a hand to the top of Dustin's

head, pushing his face harder against the lawman's nightstick. "It'll be okay, son."

"Promise me, Daddy." *Who said that?*

The door opened.

Both Dustin and Cox flinched.

"Jesus," Vasinane muttered. "We've got to get to the bottom of what's happening in this town before we all either get knocked up or go to jail."

Dustin wanted that, too. He wanted Cox to get to the bottom. Deep, deep into the very bottom.

Cox turned away and adjusted his pants.

"Did the kid tell you?"

"Same as me," Cox said.

Vasinane pulled the phone from her pocket. "I'll call the hospital."

"Hospital?!" Dustin snapped.

"It's just a precaution," Cox said. "Nothing to worry about. Just a quick checkup." He turned back around.

Dustin couldn't help looking at the man's crotch. He'd somehow managed to tame his lust, but not before it left a tiny telltale dark spot on the gray fabric. "I'll take him."

"I bet you will." Vasinane snorted, then cleared her throat. "We'll both go. I don't trust either one of us alone with him right now."

Dustin snapped his gaze to the female agent. She bit her lower lip and pulled her blazer together, covering the large erect nipples, trying to cut their way through the fabric of her blouse.

Vasinane raised her smoky hazel eyes to meet Dustin's. "Mmmm...." she shook herself, then gathered the notes and the book with the arcane symbols.

"You can't take that," Dustin said, snapping out of his horny reverie. "This is the reference section."

"Federal agents," Vasinane said. "Besides, since you came

here to check this out, I think you should read up on the way to the hospital."

"Did you find something?" Cox asked.

"If Dustin managed to perform the ritual I think he did, we're all in terrible danger. This sexual hunger we're all feeling is only going to get worse."

"Worse?" Dustin asked.

"Read on the way," Vasinane said.

"Come on." Cox held out a hand as if Dustin were a damsel that needed help from her steed.

As if in a dream, Dustin put his hand in Cox's, reveling in the big man's strength as he helped lift Dustin from his seat. "I want to be a secret agent," Dustin heard himself say from far away.

"Special Agent," Cox corrected. "You'd make a great one. I could mentor you."

"Ugh," Vasinane groaned. "Just 'cause he's legal...."

Cox chuckled. "Are you impugning my integrity, Special Agent Vasinane?"

"Perish the thought." She said.

AT THE FRONT DESK, Mrs. Wetmore shook her head when Special Agent Cox told her he'd be taking Crowley's grimoire. "Absolutely not!"

Cox gave her a gentle, pearly smile. "But Mrs. Wetmore, this is a federal investigation."

"And that, is a rare and valuable grimoire," she said, clutching the book. "You can't have it."

Cox stepped around the counter and got nose to nose with the librarian. He put his hand over hers, caressing her wrinkled fingers. "I understand," he breathed in her ear, "how much you *want* it. How desperately you *need* it."

In the quiet library, Dustin could actually hear the scrape of Cox's stubble on Wetmore's cheek.

"And when this is all over," Cox continued, "I'll *give* it to you." He punctuated the word give with a thrust of his hips, pinning Wetmore to the cash drawer.

"Oh," Wetmore moaned. "I... I... you don't understand?"

"Dick..." Vasinane warned.

Cox didn't back off. "Help me understand—" Cox glanced down at her nametag, "—Loretta."

"I... Please...." Loretta Wetmore breathed. She pressed her hips toward Cox.

Strange, angry butterflies banged against Dustin's stomach. He imagined Cox pinning *him* to the cash register.

"Loretta, you don't want to interfere with a federal investigation. Do you want to spend the weekend in... *handcuffs?*"

"Oh," Wetmore moaned.

Dustin did. Suddenly, he wanted more than anything to spend the weekend in handcuffs with Special Agent Dick Cox.

"Thank you," Cox pulled the book from Mrs. Wetmore's slack fingers, "Loretta."

OUTSIDE, Cox opened the back door of a black sedan and motioned for Dustin to get in. His perfect lips drew into a smile, exposing impossibly white teeth. "Watch your head." The Agent put a gentle hand on Dustin's head, steering it to brush against the bulge in the man's trousers.

Goddamn.

Dustin pressed a hand to his crotch once the door closed. A quarter-sized spot of pre-cum darkened his jeans right through his cotton boxers, the double layers of his pocket, and the thick denim. Fuck. They needed to solve this mystery before Dustin died of embarrassment... or blue balls.

In the rearview mirror, Vasinane winked a hazel eye at him.

She was easier for Dustin to resist. Her brusque, down to business manner put Dustin on his guard. As far as girls went though, she was very much his type: full figured and self-assured. As they drove, he kept catching her sneaking glances at him in the mirror. And, rather than freaking Dustin out, it kind of endeared her to Dustin. It was only natural. Who didn't like being adored?

The closer they got to the hospital, the more nervous Dustin became. And the more nervous he became, the less he wanted to go to the hospital. "I'm fine, you know." He met Special Agent Vasinane's eyes in the mirror. "You can just take me home."

"Don't give her any ideas," Cox said.

CHAPTER
FIVE

At the hospital, it was everything Dustin could do not to reach for Special Agent Cox's hand as they waited to be seen. Their badges had moved them to the top of the line, and instead of triage, Dustin found himself in a small, empty waiting room with the two sexy Secret Service agents. Both Vasinane and Cox kept looking at Dustin like he was a rare dessert behind a glass display case. Mouthwatering, and off limits. Or, maybe that was in his head. A dull buzzing at the back of his skull told him his perception of reality couldn't be trusted.

Had Cox pressed his pant covered erection to Dustin's face? Had the secret service man used his sexuality to get the book from the librarian? Had Vasinane covered her aroused nipples when she'd walked in on Dustin and Cox? The ghost sex? Had Mary-Jean said she'd almost fuck him?

He pinched himself. It hurt.

"Dustin Scopae?" a gorgeous dark-skinned man called.

Dustin rose and went to the door. "I'm Dustin," he said, and immediately realized that he was the only one who got up. Of course he was Dustin. Heat bloomed in his cheeks.

The nurse, who was a head taller than Dustin, looked down and winked a big, kind eye. "Gotcha. I'm Peter." He held the door open with a heavily muscled arm that looked like it might rip through the sleeve of his scrubs. "This way."

There was no way of ignoring the way Nurse Peter's rock hard bubble butt filled out his scrubs as he led Dustin to the examination room.

"Okay," Peter gestured to a room on the right, "we'll be in here. Please undress and put on the gown. I'll be back in a minute to take your vitals, and then we'll head for the CT scan."

"Undress... all the way?" Dustin asked. He wasn't a prude, but he was afraid of what might happen if Nurse Peter touched him... down there.

The nurse smiled, nodded, and closed the door.

Dustin changed into the gown and sat on the exam table with the paper crinkling under his bare bottom. Maybe he shouldn't have worried. The exam room's chill air and Dustin's nervous energy might conspire to keep his reactions small.

A gentle knock sounded. Before Dustin could find his voice, Peter came back in. God, he was perfect. His tight curls were cropped close to his scalp, with perfectly sculpted lines at his temples and forehead. Not a single blemish marked his skin, so perfect and black that the man might have been carved from onyx or obsidian. The gentleness of Peter's touch surprised Dustin, as the ebony Adonis slipped the blood pressure cuff into place, raising goosebumps on Dustin's skin.

Unbidden, images of Dustin curling up in Peter's arms marched across his imagination. Dustin closed his eyes. In his mind, the blood pressure cuff became Peter's iron grip, pulling Dustin to him. He pressed a hand to Peter's chest, feeling the soft skin over Peter's hard, chiseled pecs.

Peter's voice broke Dustin from his reverie.

"Okay, your blood pressure is a little elevated. Not too much, but are you stressed or excited right now?"

"Yes," Dustin said a little too quickly. Besides the ghost egg that might be inside him, there was Special Agent Dreamy, and Nurse Yes Please.

Peter's full, delicious lips parted to reveal a kind, white smile. "That's understandable. Hop up on the scale, please."

Dustin did his best to hunch over so his gown would billow out around his burgeoning erection as he climbed down from the exam table and stepped over to the scale.

Knob Hill's tiny hospital didn't have fancy new digital scales. Instead, Nurse Peter stood at Dustin's elbow, peppermint breath making a gentle tickling breeze on Dustin's cheek as he tapped the scale's weights with practiced, graceful motions.

The rest of the visit went about the same as any hospital visit might, with the notable exception of the crackling energy between Dustin and Peter as the nurse took his medical history and led him back and forth from the CT scan.

When it was all done, Nurse Peter stood in the exam room slightly closer than professionalism would normally allow. "I know I'm not supposed to ask, but I noticed you came in with those people in the suits. And, the way you got moved to the top of the triage list...." The big man's words faltered.

Dustin got that pins and needles sensation in the back of his skull again. He leaned in toward Peter. "Yes?"

Peter met his eyes. The galaxy swirled in the nurse's dark irises. "Can you tell me what's going on in this town? Everyone feels so...."

"Horny," Dustin finished for him. Their lips only inches apart.

"Horny," Peter agreed in a husky whisper. Dustin inched closer.

Peter did too.

Their lips met. Soft. Tender flesh on flesh.

Peter pulled away. "I'm sorry. That was unprofessional."

"No." Dustin put a hand on the rippling shoulder muscles hidden by Peter's tan scrubs. "That was my fault." He stepped back. "I don't know what's going on exactly, but we're working on it."

Peter gave a faint smile. "Hurry up, before I lose control. Lose my job."

"We're doing our best," Dustin said. "Can you tell me what the CT scan showed?"

"I didn't see the results," Peter said. "The doctor will be in to discuss it. Goodbye Dustin."

Dustin let his hand trail down Peter's arm, feeling the muscle as he went. When his fingers reached Peter's hand, he gave it a squeeze.

THE DOCTOR DIDN'T COME in. Instead, Cox came to get Dustin.

"What were my CT scan results?" Dustin asked.

Cox turned away. "Don't worry about it."

The fuck? "No one says that unless there's something to worry about."

"Not right now," Cox said. "Come on, we've figured some stuff out."

CHAPTER
SIX

Dustin kicked the back of Cox's seat. "I still want to know my CT scan results!"

"You're fine," Vasinane said from behind the wheel of the government issue black sedan. "Now shut up and listen. Crowley's book describes a ritual for bringing back the dead where someone travels around the inside of a circle. A circle with very specific symbols and words written on it. It says that anyone inside the circle will be affected by the spell. Compelled to have sex with the dead. And after—"

Cox elbowed Vasinane.

"After, *what*?" Dustin insisted.

"We have to tell him," Vasinane said.

Cox rubbed his face. "Fine. Fuck it." He turned in his seat and looked at Dustin. "And afterward, the person will grow a body for the ghost."

"Uh...." It sounded like an agent of the federal government had just told Dustin he might be growing a ghost body.

"Yeah." Cox made a wry face. "Look. You and I are the only ones to have this experience, that will admit to it. But the whole town is horny as fuck. So, we think anyone who does the circle road reactivates the ritual."

"Yeah," Dustin said, "But there'd have to be writing...." He remembered Mrs. Wetmore collecting fucking oak galls for special ink.

"There's no writing, Dustin. We've looked."

Dustin took out his phone, opened the browser, and searched oak gall ink.

"What're you doing?" Cox asked.

"Solving your case," Dustin said.

"Not a moment too soon," Vasinane said.

"Yeah," Dustin said, "graduation's in a few days."

"No, it's not that. I'm so fucking horny we've got to solve this thing before I do something..." Vasinane trailed off.

Dustin looked up from his phone. Vasinane made eye contact in the mirror and licked her lips.

"We need to go to Missus Wetmore's house," Dustin said.

"Why?" Vasinane and Cox asked at once.

"Because, if I'm right, she's the one who did the ritual." Dustin smiled and leaned back in the seat. His cock stirred. Seriously, solving this case was giving him a boner.

"Tell us," Cox said.

"What were my CT scan results?" Dustin countered.

"This again?" Vasinane asked.

"Yes," Dustin said, "this again. You tell me what's in-fucking-side me, and I'll tell you what we'll find at our dear aged librarian's house."

"There's a mass in your stomach," Cox said. "Same as mine. And just like mine, yours can't be removed because it has blood vessels all through your stomach. Now, if we can undo this ritual, I believe it will kill the ghost seed inside us. So, let's fucking hurry, okay?"

Dustin felt his stomach drop, and churn, and try to exit his mouth. Blood rushed to his head. He leaned forward and put his head between his knees. "Oh god."

"I told you not to worry about it," Cox said. "It's going to be okay."

"How do you know?" Dustin's voice sounded small and far away even to himself.

"Because I've got years of experience with this shit, Dustin. And I've got you, and you cracked the case. So, spill."

"Oh, yes," Vasinane moaned, "spill, you handsome young man, spill, spill."

"Are you jacking off right now?" Cox asked.

"M-maybe," Vasinane grunted.

"Get your hand out of your pants and drive the car," Cox said.

Somewhere between the spell on the town, and the pheromones in the car, Dustin lost interest in his stomach, and found a renewed pull toward his crotch. He pressed a hand to his cock, straining against his pants.

"Oh my God," Cox said, taking in the view of Dustin touching himself through the stretched denim. "Dustin, tell us the deal before we drive off the road or get lost in some weird orgy sex magic."

"I...ugh," Dustin wanted to take his dick out so bad. "I saw Mrs. Wetmore by the side of the road. She was collecting oak galls—"

"Oak balls?" Vasinane moaned.

"Galls," Dustin corrected. "She said she was trying to make medieval ink. But, those galls can also be used to make invisible ink."

"How do you know this shit?" Cox asked.

"A little thing called the internet," Dustin said. "And we can make the ink appear with the right reagent."

"What reagent?" Vasinane asked.

"Seriously," Cox said, "Special Agent Vasinane, get your hand out of your pants. I can't believe of the three of us, I'm the one acting like I'm not a horny teenager."

"I am a horny teenager," Dustin said.

"Mmmmm...." Vasinane moaned.

"Vasinane, STOP IT. Dustin, you stop too. Now, what's the fucking reagent?"

"Depending on how she made the ink, it could be a couple of things. But, we'll know if we find a shitload of the chemical at her house."

Cox SPENT the remainder of the trip describing what he imagined it would look like if Winston Churchill and Betty White played naked baseball. By the time they arrived at Mrs. Wetmore's house, Dustin's self lust was reduced to aching balls and a semi that made it only slightly uncomfortable to walk.

The old cape house stood at the end of a short dead-end street next to the cemetery. As they went up the front steps, the sound of a woman screaming deep inside the house became audible.

Cox and Vasinane drew their guns.

"Stay back," Cox put a gentle hand on Dustin's chest, sending chills chasing up and down his spine.

Vasinane stood on one side of the front door, Cox on the other.

"Federal Agents!" Cox yelled. "Open up!"

They waited. No one came to the door.

Vasinane tried the handle.

The door opened.

They went in, guns first, one by one.

Dustin couldn't see into the interior of the house. And, he sure as fuck wasn't about to stand around on the front walk. He was the one who'd directed them here. And he was certain he was the one who cracked the case. After a few eternal seconds, Dustin followed the Secret Service agents into the house.

In the front hall, Cox swung around, almost slapping Dustin with the gun. "I thought I told you to wait outside," he whispered.

Dustin shrugged.

"Goddamnit," Cox whispered.

The screaming continued, only now inside where it was louder, two voices were clear, a man and a woman. The agents followed the noise down the hall to the left of the kitchen. As Dustin passed, he saw jugs of liquid iron plant fertilizer on the kitchen table. More than a dozen home gardeners could use in a year. In that moment, he was certain he'd solved the case. But Dustin had a new mystery begging for answers: who was making Loretta Wetmore scream like that, and, how were they doing it. The answer lay at the end of the hall.

"Give it to me, Reggie!" Mrs. Wetmore screamed.

Dustin, Vasinane, and Cox exchanged looks.

"There goes probable cause," Vasinane whispered.

"In for a penny," Cox said.

They advanced down the hall, with Vasinane in the lead. When she arrived in the doorway, Vasinane stood frozen, gun pointed into the room.

"Don't just stand there," a male voice growled, "come join us."

"Agent Vasinane," Mrs. Wetmore's voice grunted, "what are you doing here?"

"We heard screaming," Vasinane said, holstering her pistol.

"Special Agent Vasinane," Cox hissed. He advanced to the doorway, leaving Dustin standing alone in the hall.

"Oh," Dustin said.

"I have to admit, Reggie, the audience is turning me on," Mrs. Wetmore managed between moans.

Dustin wasn't stupid. He knew what was going on in the room, and though he didn't find Mrs. Wetmore attractive, he did want to know who the fuck Reggie was. Elbowing Cox aside, Dustin stood in the doorway between the Secret Service agents. In front of him, Mrs. Wetmore kneeled on the bed, ass in the air, while the shimmering blue ghost of her late husband Reginald held her hips as he thrust deep inside her.

"Hi, Dustin," she smiled. "Like what you see?"

Dustin did. Her perfect alabaster skin glowed with ghostly youth. Her full breasts swayed underneath her, their rigid tips grazing the sheets as she moved. "I...yes," he replied.

"You can see mine," her eyes locked on the bulge in Dustin's pants. "Show me yours. I've always wondered what made your trousers tent."

As if in a trance, Dustin unbuttoned his pants and took out his rapidly stiffening cock.

"Dustin! No...." Special Agent Vasinane's words trailed off when she saw the hard slab of teen meat in Dustin's hand. "Don't..." But Vasinane's hands weren't taking the advice her mouth was sending. Instead, one hand pinched the outline of a nipple through her blouse. The other snaked down underneath the waist of her skirt.

Dustin glanced in Cox's direction. The handsome agent had his cock out, too. It rivaled Dustin's own in size. And it was as if someone had copied the Roman ideal of a chiseled marble penis and stuck it on Cox's body. Dustin looked into Cox's big, beautiful eyes and reached out his hand.

"You shouldn't," Cox whispered.

"I want to," Dustin said as his fingers wrapped around the velvety skin of Cox's big, beautiful dick.

"Fuck, that's hot," Vasinane said, stepping out of her skirt and panties. She took up a position facing both Mrs. Wetmore and the two men she'd entered with. Her hand rubbed circles on the dark thatch of hair between her legs while her eyes darted from the ghost sex to her left and the homoerotic spectacle to her right.

Dustin had never seen a woman masturbate before, and it turned him on almost as much as stroking the strong Secret Service Agent's cock.

"Oh, that feels so good, Dustin." Cox put his arm out and pulled Dustin to his side.

The warmth of Cox's body and the reassuring arm around him made Dustin feel so safe and loved that he inadvertently sped up his strokes on Cox's dick.

Mrs. Wetmore stared at Dustin and licked her lips. "I want to taste that delicious young cock."

Though Loretta Wetmore had transformed in Dustin's mind from an old dry librarian into a sexy mature creature, he didn't want to leave the warmth of Agent Cox's arms, and the strong dominant energy and amazing feel of the agent's throbbing weapon.

"You're getting yours," Vasinane said to Loretta. She stripped off her blazer, blouse, and bra and advanced on Dustin. "What do you say, Dustin? You cracked the case. Care to leave some evidence inside me?"

"It's a spell, Trish," Cox said. "Sex magic, remember?"

"Look who's talking. He's got your dick in his hand. He might as well put *his* to use... in me." She climbed onto the bed facing Loretta and wiggled her round, firm bottom. "Come on, Dustin."

"Look at them, Reggie!" Loretta moaned. "Look what we've done! Look at all this happiness and horniness. Oh, fuck me, Reggie!"

"Do me Dustin!" the female agent moaned.

Special Agent Trish Vasinane wiggled her ass and stared at Dustin with smoky eyes.

But Dustin was right where he wanted to be. Where he needed to be. In the arms of a tall, strong, Special Agent, and suddenly Dustin wanted the sexy Cox to earn his name. And even though he'd never been with a guy before, a magic induced bravery pumped through Dustin's veins. He squeezed Cox's nightstick and led the lawman out of the room.

"Hey!" Vasinane called, disappointed.

CHAPTER
SEVEN

In the next room, Dustin let go of the Special Agent's cock and closed the door by leaning up against it. He reached up with a trembling hand and grabbed a fistful of the short hair on the back of Cox's head, pulling the taller man's lips to his own.

Cox's rough, dark, five o'clock shadow grazed against Dustin's tender lips. The taller man's arms came around Dustin. His hands pried Dustin from the door and wrapped around him, meeting and then crossing behind Dustin's back.

Lips parted, Dustin leaned in, his tongue seeking out its mate in Cox's mouth. And when he found it, they danced a wet, sensual waltz behind the lawman's perfect white teeth.

Dustin squirmed against Cox, begging with his lithe, youthful body for the lawman to lose control and give him the serious dicking down he needed. Strange. Until today, he hadn't really given guys that much thought. And, he couldn't tell for sure if it was the spell from Crowley's book, or the incredible, sexy Federal Agent, but either way, Dustin had never wanted a woman the way he wanted Special Agent Dick Cox.

As if sensing Dustin's thoughts, Cox took Dustin in his arms and carried him to the daybed.

Dustin lay gazing up as Dick tossed his sport coat aside and started to remove the shoulder holster. "Don't."

Cox frowned down at him. "You want the cop fantasy, Dustin? We could do that, and it would be great. But you're the sexiest creature under the stars, and I want to connect with you soul to soul. That would be a thousand times sexier than cocks and robbers."

Dustin couldn't help giggling. "Good one," he said. "Take off the gun."

"That's my young man."

At those words, Dustin, already erect and dripping in his pants, stiffened into an iron bar. He lay still while Cox undressed above him and stared with smoky lust at Dustin.

"Take off your shoes," Dick Cox commanded.

Dustin did. Awkwardly. Never lifting his shoulders from the bed. All the while watching the white fabric of Cox's shirt part to reveal a dark chest with cut muscles and sparse black hair.

"Good job," Cox said. "Unbuckle your belt."

Dick unbuckled his, then pulled his jutting cock back through his fly, unbuttoned his pants and let them drop to the floor. Then his boxers. Cox's perfectly sculpted penis popped out again and pointed at Dustin like a baseball player calling his next home run, bat extended.

Dustin sat up. His eyes locked with Cox's as his lips parted and his tongue darted out, caressing the tip of the lawman's cock. The salty, tangy, pre-cum at its tip sent Dustin into a pheromone frenzy. Dustin used the moisture, adding it to his salivating mouth, and sucked Cox's cock deep, until it bumped the back of his throat.

The Special Agent grabbed a fistful of Dustin's hair. Then pulled him back, driving Dustin forward again with just enough force that Dustin felt safe and yet absolutely certain what the tall, dark lawman wanted of him.

He reached out, gently stroking Cox's balls, running his fingertips along the velvety skin. Weighing them, feeling their masculine essence.

Cox withdrew his dick from Dustin's mouth. "I want to kiss you more, and undress you."

Dustin nodded.

Cox grabbed the hem of Dustin's shirt and slid it up his chest, prompting Dustin to lift his arms. He tossed the shirt and trailed his fingers along Dustin's chest, pushing him down into the daybed. Cox had the button and zipper of Dustin's jeans open so fast Dustin wondered if they trained for that at Quantico. And with a quick dive in and a kiss, Cox yanked Dustin's pants down.

The Federal Agent sent Dustin's pants tumbling across the room. Then, seized with animal lust, Cox grabbed Dustin's ankles and hoisted them atop his shoulders. He rubbed the tip against Dustin's opening, smearing his copious excitement in all the right places. His big brown eyes never broke from Dustin's. Boring into him, expressing desire and intent.

Dustin didn't move. Didn't speak, making the Alpha above him wait. Driving Cox wild with excitement and need.

Cox bumped gently against Dustin, one centimeter further, each time. His nightstick kissing Dustin's opening with need, gentle but insistent. Until just one hair's breadth more would unite the two in passion.

Dustin gave the slightest nod, then closed his eyes. He shivered in ecstasy as Cox gently pushed his length inside. Delicious sensations spread up from the point of union.

"You okay?" Cox asked, sliding his fingers over Dustin's cheek and tugging Dustin's mouth open to receive a fingertip.

Dustin opened his eyes. He nodded again, sucking the Secret Agent's finger into his hungry mouth.

They moved in slow harmony. Each pushed toward the other. Trading energy. Giving and receiving grace, skin on skin, soul to soul.

Dustin had no sensation of time. The world slipped away. There existed only this handsome man, filling him, pushing his will deep inside Dustin.

"I want you to feel my passion," Cox said, leaning down and withdrawing his salty finger from Dustin's mouth. "But I don't want to hurt you. You're so precious."

"I want it," Dustin moaned. He gripped Cox's neck and pulled. But the lawman didn't budge, allowing Dustin to lift his body off the cushions.

"Oh, you dirty boy," Cox said, straightening and taking Dustin with him. He carried Dustin, hands under Dustin's thighs, to the wall. There, he banged Dustin's back to the cold floral wallpaper and thrust hard and fast.

The wind rushed out of Dustin's lungs with the simultaneous impact of the wall on his back and Cox's heavy balls on his ass. When he had his breath back, he moaned insensible words as Cox hammered into him. The ferocity of the Special Agent's thrusts sent Dustin's throbbing cock bouncing and ricocheting between their firm hairy bellies, driving Dustin mad with lust and the need to cum.

"Take it," Cox grunted, firing into Dustin like a machine gun on full auto.

"Give it to me," Dustin moaned. The sensations below his waist, front and back, overwhelmed Dustin until he spilled over between them, coating their bellies in excitement's sticky manifestation.

"Yes!" Cox growled between clenched teeth. He drove

Dustin into the wall so hard the plaster cracked with a pop, as Cox did the same inside Dustin.

The pulsing cock inside him sent shivers through Dustin as the wave of their passion crested and rolled back.

He leaned forward, opening his mouth.

Cox obliged, giving Dustin his lips and tongue to taste as he sagged in satisfaction.

When their kiss broke, so did the spell.

"I shouldn't have," Cox said, red-faced. But he didn't move. He didn't let Dustin down.

"I'm glad you did." Dustin leaned in again, giving Cox another kiss, shy and closed mouthed.

Cox smiled. Then, his face fell. "Shit. I left Vasinane alone with a ghost cocksman!"

Dustin nodded. "We should check."

They cleaned and dressed quickly, the only evidence of their passing a scrap of fabric Mrs. Wetmore probably wouldn't use for anything else.

In the bedroom, Special Agent Vasinane lay on the bed as Mrs. Wetmore rode her face and pulled her hair. Vasinane's legs flopped in the crook of the handsome ghost's elbows as he fucked her, standing at the edge of the bed.

"Yes, take it," Mrs. Wetmore moaned. "Take the seed! Fertilize it, Reggie!"

As one, Dustin and Cox dashed forward. Dustin shoved the librarian away, knocking her onto the bed. Cox pushed the ghost back, just in time for the ghosts seed to spatter uselessly all over Vasinane's belly and dark, silver dollar nipples.

"You cock blocking assholes!" Vasinane wailed.

But Dustin and Cox weren't paying attention to her. Instead, their eyes were glued to the small, gray egg that popped out of Mrs. Wetmore's sex and lay vibrating on the white comforter.

"NO!" Wetmore screamed. She leaped up and began scooping the ghost's cum off Vasinane's belly and smearing it all over the egg.

Vasinane grabbed Wetmore's wrist too late. With her other hand, Wetmore pushed the slimy egg inside herself. "Well, you two could literally fuck up a wet dream."

Vasinane flopped back, gasping. "I didn't get to finish."

"We have to undo the ritual," Cox said.

Vasinane puffed out a breath. "It's never about the woman."

"It's always about the woman," the ghost said. He began to flicker.

"Why are the good ones always dead?" Vasinane lamented, getting up.

"Tell me about it," Wetmore said. "That's what I was trying to fix until you...."

"Meddling kids?" Dustin added hopefully.

"Quiet, Dustin," Wetmore said. "The grownups are talking."

Anger burned in Dustin's cheeks. "Cool," he said. "Well, since the kitchen is stuffed with the reagent for your invisible writing, I'm going out to Circle Road to undo the spell. You *adults* can stay here jerking off." He walked out of the room.

CHAPTER
EIGHT

By the time Dustin filled his arms with iron fertilizer jugs, Vasinane and Cox appeared at his side, slightly disheveled.

"So, mister bigshot," Vasinane said, a little annoyed, "what's your plan?"

"Well, I flipped through Crowley's book on the ride over here," Dustin said. "And I think all we have to do is break the circle."

"How?" Vasinane asked, adjusting her blouse.

"We use the reagent to find the writing, because there's no way she covered the outside circumference. Once we find it, we have to scratch out the particular phrase summoning the ghosts. I marked it in the book.

"What else do we need?" Cox asked.

"Water," Dustin said.

Outside, thunder rolled.

"Might not be a problem," Vasinane said.

· · ·

VASINANE DROVE, and being the small town it was, they were on Circle Road in minutes. As the first fat drops of rain fell on the parched pavement, Vasinane pulled off to the side.

Dustin uncapped the iron, spattering it between the white line and the edge where the pavement met the oak forest.

As the rain came, the writing became clear. Vasinane held the book, working to match the arcane symbols drawn on the pavement with the ones in the book. "Here!" she pointed.

Cox stood over her shoulder, holding the umbrella, shielding the grimoire from the rain.

"Okay," Dustin said. "This is the one we need to erase." He pointed to a string of characters about a quarter of the way around the circle.

Vasinane snapped the book shut.

Since leaving Mrs. Wetmore's house, a pit had been growing in Dustin's stomach. A sadness he didn't understand seeped into his consciousness. It wasn't until Cox caught his arm as he opened the car door, that Dustin realized what these strange new feelings were about. Just the simple skin contact, hand to arm, made the existential sorrow recede. He looked down. "I'm okay."

"Dustin," Cox said. He lifted Dustin's chin. "Make space for yourself in this world. If you need something, you have to ask."

"Would you sit with me?" Dustin asked in a small voice.

"Of course," Cox said.

"Hey what're you—" Vasinane started.

Cox made a cutting motion with his hand.

Vasinane shrugged and got behind the wheel.

In the back seat, Cox closed Dustin's hand inside his.

The pit in Dustin's stomach filled in.

Vasinane pulled over a few minutes later. "Okay, this is about ninety degrees. It should be somewhere around here." She got out.

Cox opened the door.

Dustin caught the Secret Service man's arm and screwed up his courage. "Kiss me."

Cox leaned toward him and gave him a gentle peck on the lips. He held Dustin's gaze for a moment. "Always make sure you ask for the aftercare you need." He smiled, gave Dustin's hand a parting squeeze, and got out of the car.

IT TOOK THREE TRIES, walking along the roadside in the rain and splashing the fertilizer on the pavement to find the phrase they needed to erase.

"So, how do we do it?" Cox asked. "The fertilizer isn't making the writing disappear."

"I think we can just cross it out," Dustin said. Really, he was talking out of his ass. "Maybe smashing some oak galls across the symbols. He stepped to the forest's edge. The leaves dripped onto Dustin, cooling his burning need for Cox's touch.

Dustin showed the others how and where to find the oak galls. Soon all three were stomping the big green orbs into the blacktop and smearing the juices across the symbols. It took almost half an hour of trips to strike a line through the phrase on the pavement.

And when Vasinane smeared the last gall, lightning struck the street, sending all three flying into the grass.

"Everyone all right?" Cox asked, rubbing uselessly at the mud on his suit.

"I'm okay," Dustin called, getting up. He noticed immediately the burning awareness of his cock that had grown over the last days was gone.

"I think it worked," Vasinane said.

"It worked," Cox agreed. The look he gave Dustin brought a

lump to the young man's throat. "I'm sorry, Dustin, I've acted unprofessionally."

"Me too," Vasinane agreed. Her face went crimson.

"You're *sorry*?" Dustin crossed his arms. "So, what? I'm a fucking mistake? Is that it?"

"Dustin...." Cox held out a hand.

Dustin turned and checked his phone, just to give him something to do. "Take me to my car."

Cox headed for the back seat again, but Dustin slammed the door before he got there. No one spoke on the way back to the library.

NINE

With no time to go home and change, and with his clothes absolutely soaked and filthy, Dustin had no choice but to walk the stage and get his diploma, commando. His cock swung heavily back and forth under his robes as he took the sheepskin and shook the principal's hand.

With all the activity and nervousness of starting his adult life in earnest, Dustin didn't have time to dwell on his feelings about what happened with Special Agent Cox. He took pictures with his mom, he spoke with his few nerdy friends. And when the festivities wound down, he found Cox and Vasinane standing in the corner of the gym, taking in the festivities.

Dustin sucked in a breath, then let it out slowly and approached the Secret Service Agents.

"Congratulations," Vasinane said, pulling Dustin into a hug.

Dustin held his arms out to Cox, who extended a hand instead.

Dustin took it, looking at his feet.

Cox pulled him in close. "I don't trust myself around you, Dustin. You're not a mistake. You're a continuing temptation.

That spell didn't make me attracted to you. It made me act on that attraction. And I shouldn't have. As a man of conscience. You're too young, and I'm a professional. I'm sorry I hurt you. I'm not sorry that I made love to you."

Dustin pushed him back and nodded. Not what he wanted. And, he couldn't pretend he wasn't hurt, but at least now he understood. "So what now? Back to Washington?"

"One last thing," Cox frowned. "We've all got to go back to the hospital."

"Why?" Dustin asked, but then, something in his gut that wasn't part of him, kicked.

"Ghost babies," Cox said.

"My CT scan results?" Dustin asked.

Cox nodded.

CHAPTER

TEN

Luckily retrieving the egg from inside Dustin didn't require surgery, but the process was both unpleasant and undignified. If the technician noticed evidence of Cox's invasion of Dustin's backside, he was professional enough not to comment.

"Can I see?" Dustin asked.

"Best not to," the tech said.

Again, a pit formed in Dustin's stomach. A deep sense of loss stole over his consciousness. As if they'd taken more than just some extra-dimensional artifact from Dustin, but a part of himself. A part he might spend the rest of his life searching for.

Outside the hospital, Dustin stood with Cox and Vasinane between their parked cars. The rain had stopped, and a glistening rainbow draped itself across the sky.

"I have questions," Dustin said. "If Mrs. Wetmore was trying to summon the ghost of her husband, where did all the other ghosts come from? And what was all the egg business? And why did they put them inside us?"

Vasinane and Cox gave each other a look, but said nothing.

"It's classified," Vasinane said.

"Oh, come *on!*"

"Sorry." It was Cox's turn to look at the ground.

"I'll give you two a minute," Vasinane said. She swept Dustin into a strong embrace. "You did good, kid. Congratulations. Thanks for helping us solve the case." She released him, climbed into the car, and turned on the radio.

"Can't you tell me?" Dustin asked. "I helped you solve this thing."

Cox looked uncomfortable. "I wish I could."

A lump formed in Dustin's throat, despite his indignation. There were a lot more emotions in play here. "I wish you could stay."

Cox put his arms around Dustin, rocking him gently. "Girls fall in love, then have sex. Guys have sex, then fall in love. But, I'm not *for* you Dustin. Someday you'll find a person who completes you. Who is your best friend and your lover. That's how you'll know."

Dustin said nothing.

"I'm amazingly proud of you. And, grateful for your help solving this case. I think you should come work with us when you get out of college. You're good at this. Then maybe you can find out what this was *really* all about."

That idea gave Dustin a spark of hope. Maybe in four years he could go to Washington, and work with Cox. By then, maybe Cox would consider him old enough to take as a lover, or... husband. "How do I do that?"

"Study hard," Cox whispered in Dustin's ear. "Study criminal justice, philosophy, religion, the occult, and then come see me for a job."

"I will," Dustin said.

And, he did.

THE WOLFMAN OF NOTTING HOLLOW

A SHORT, STEAMY, QUEER, MONSTER
ROMANCE

CHAPTER
ONE

Cade Woodman stomped through the forest, fists clenched, breath steaming into the cold autumn air. Something big rustled in the trees ahead of him. Cade didn't care. If it was a bear, he'd just as soon let it eat him. But the noise receded ahead of him. Whatever it was, he must have scared it off.

Cade wasn't really paying attention to where he was going. Instead, his mind replayed the argument he'd had with his boyfriend as John shoved his hastily packed belongings into his car. Cade couldn't think of much to say on the spur of the moment, so, he'd stormed off.

It wasn't Cade's fault. He was a quiet, pensive man. But now, tromping through the West Virginia pine forest high in the mountains, he could think of plenty of things to say. He'd say that maybe if John spent less time cruising Grindr and the porn sites, and a little more time paying attention to Cade, their sex life wouldn't have died. He'd say that his silence came from being a pensive writer. He'd say that John only loved him for his boyish face and fit body anyway. He'd say.... Well, what did it matter now? John was gone, and Cade would never feel John's soft lips on his again. Never sigh with pleasure when John dragged his stubbled chin across the nape of Cade's neck, sending shivers down his spine. All that was gone.

Pine needles crunched under Cade's boots. The trees closed in around him. And still he kept going, pushing branches out of his way with impatient hands, not allowing the forest to break his angry stride. Again, he replayed the scene back at his house, John's cruel words. John loading the car. The whole time, traveling deeper and deeper into the vast forest of the Smoky Mountains.

As Cade's anger cooled and his rational mind came back to the fore, he slowed his pace. Darkness crept into the corners of the sky visible through the pine boughs. Time to turn around. Except, which way was home? The thick and swollen clouds loomed with the promise of snow. Cade had left the house with only his parka. No hat. No gloves. No phone. Worst of all, as familiar as he was with the woods around his house, Cade didn't recognize this place at all. The forest had a strange humpish quality, as if some secret were buried underneath.

A mad, desperate howl, long and low, echoed through the hills. Too deep for a wolf, and, wolves hadn't been reintroduced here. But man, if it was a coyote, it was a really goddamned big one. Cade wasn't easily spooked, but he didn't want to meet whatever made that sound. Not without a rifle. He did his best to judge from what direction the call came, and headed the other way. Down. When in doubt, in these mountains, down was always the best choice. If nothing else, at least the weather would be milder. Usually, though, you could find a road after a while.

The darkness closed in tighter as the monstrous howl sounded again. Cade looked back up into the hills. A branch slapped him in the face. He turned forward just in time to see the cliff.

Cade stopped short.

The ground fell away under his feet.

The bottom fell out of Cade's stomach as the ground rushed up to meet him.

CHAPTER
TWO

Agonizing pain in Cade's leg brought him back to consciousness. His head pounded. With cold-numb fingers, Cade reached down, exploring the agony in his leg. Cold, crystalline dust met his grasp, crusted on his jeans. When Cade opened his eyes, he was greeted by moonlight on a glistening dusting of snow covering everything. When he looked down at his body, he wished he hadn't. Cade's left leg lay twisted at an unnatural angle. Not good. He tried to straighten it... and screamed in pain.

When Cade tried to sit up an intense wave of nausea took him. He fell back. Even with his writer's vocabulary, the only word he could think of to describe his situation was: fucked. He was so fucked. John certainly wasn't going to come looking for him. His next publishing deadline wasn't for two months, and his friends were all in other states. At best, it might be a week before someone got worried that he wasn't answering his phone or email. John was his whole world. A world gone now.

"So," he whispered to the soft flakes falling on his thick lashes, "this is how I end." And then a minute later. "No. Get it together, Cade. Get up, splint the leg, and find shelter."

Cade tried to sit up again, and passed out.

HE CAME TO WITH A SCREAM. Something yanked his broken leg. A blanket was draped over his head. Another yank on his leg. And again, Cade passed out, this time from the pain.

When Cade came back to himself, a small fire crackled by his elbow. His head lay on a cushion of pine branches. And to his amazement, a mug sat steaming by his hand.

"What the—" Cade jerked upright and almost threw up.

"Easy," a deep voice growled in the shadows. "You've had a pretty rough day."

"Who's there?" Cade craned his neck and squinted into the trees behind him.

"A friend," the voice said.

"Wouldn't a friend be sitting by the fire with me?"

"Would an enemy splint your leg, build a fire, and fix you cocoa?" the gruff voice countered.

"cocoa?" Cade stared at the cup. "Really?"

"Why not?" the voice said.

"What...." There were just too many questions.

"Drink the cocoa," the deep voice commanded.

"Why?"

"Ugh," the voice grunted. "Because it's fucking cold, and I don't want you to go into shock. It's a miracle you're in as good a shape as you are."

Cade shook his head, trying to clear the cobwebs — and instantly regretted it. The world wobbled sickly around him. "Oh, God."

"Don't be stubborn. Drink the cocoa."

"Why are you hiding?" Cade asked. He touched a hand to the back of his head. It came away sticky with congealed blood. Something tickled the back of Cade's addled brain. And no, it wasn't the wound. Tracks. There were no tracks in the dusting of snow. Instead, there were scuff marks, as if someone swept the area with a branch. "You wiped away your tracks."

"You're delirious. Those marks are from where I dragged the branches your head was resting on."

Plausible, but, definitely bullshit in Cade's estimation. "I'm not buying what you're selling."

"Why do you people always have to make everything trans-actional?" the voice growled.

"You people?"

"Do you want to lay here in the snow all night, or do you want to drink the cocoa so I can take you somewhere warm?"

"No way." Cade caught himself before he shook his head. Bad idea. "Not until you tell me why you're hiding, and why you want me to drink this cocoa so badly."

"Fuck it. Okay. I'm kind of unusual, and shy. But I wasn't about to let you die out here. The cocoa has some pain reliever and a sedative in it so it won't hurt as much when I move you. And also, so you won't freak out when you see me."

Cade looked at the steaming cup. He *was* cold, thirsty, and in pain. He took the handle, raised it to his lips, and stared out at the spot the voice came from.

"I promise, I won't harm you. If that was my intent, you'd already be harmed," the gruff voice asserted.

Cade took a tentative sip. The cocoa was good. Made from water, not milk, obviously, but still. And, it did have a bit of a medicine aftertaste. He rubbed his tongue on the roof of his mouth, trying to place it.

"Go on," the voice said. Its tone was much softer now, like a doctor or a nurse trying to get Cade to take his medicine.

Cade drank greedily. The warmth traveled down his throat to his belly. He set the mug down. "There. Happy?"

"I was never unhappy. Just concerned."

"Can I see what you look like now?" Cade asked.

"In due time," the voice said. "Lie back. Once the medicine kicks in, I'll get you out of here."

"To where?" Cade asked, already feeling sleepy.

"My place."

"How far...."

THREE

The world bounced in darkness.

Footfalls crunched in the snow. They weren't Cade's.

Whoever carried him smelled pleasantly of pine tar and beeswax. Another scent, familiar and elusive, just wouldn't coalesce in Cade's addled brain. He opened his eyes. His face was buried in soft fabric. A sweatshirt. It took another moment to orient himself. He was slung over someone's shoulder. He raised his head. Snow still fell into the dark, silent forest. Cade could just make out the shape of the tracks trailing away behind them. That was.... They were... not right. The effort to hold up his head and think was too much.

Cade fell into darkness.

When he woke up again, cotton-headed and thirsty, the first thing Cade noticed was the warmth. The second, was the humidity. Beads of sweat stood out on his forehead and dripped down into his hair.

Somewhere close by, water trickled into a pool. The echoes it made hinted at a small space. When Cade tried to open his eyes, he found they were already open. He waved a hand in front of his face. Nothing. His leg throbbed. So did his head. "Hello?"

"So, sleeping beauty," the voice said, "welcome back to the waking world."

"Where are we?" Cade asked.

"My house," the voice said.

"I can't help feeling you're fucking with me. Literally keeping me in the dark. Not letting me see you. I don't even know your fucking name. I want a light. I want a phone. I want a hospital. And for fuck's sake, I want a bathroom."

"Huh," the voice said. "You're kind of a bitch, aren't you?"

"Are you fucking kidding me? Look, if you brought me here to eat me, or torture me, or fuck me or something, can we get that part over with? This gaslighting thing is getting really old."

The voice chuckled. "Well, you do look delicious, but not the way you're thinking, handsome." There was a noise that sounded like panting for a moment. "My name's Max. I don't have a phone. I don't have a bathroom, at least not for elimination, that's for outside. As for baths, you're sort of in my bathroom, literally. It's eighteen miles to the closest road, and about five miles to the closest house — yours. But it's the middle of the night, and I'm not inclined to walk that with you over my shoulder. Let's deal with first things first. Do you need onsies or twosies?"

"What are you, fucking six years old? Seriously? Onsies or twosies?"

Cade could almost hear Max shrug. "That's the question alright."

"I've gotta take a piss."

"Onsies then. Easier. I'll get you a bucket. That way you can just roll on your side and you won't have to do anything... less dignified."

"I can get up—"

"On your broken leg? Go for it."

"Get me some goddamn light!"

"I'm not ready for that step."

"Well, I fucking am!" Cade shouted. His voice thundered in the enclosed space.

"Ugh, fine!" the huffed exclamation was accompanied by footsteps muffled by dirt or sand.

Somewhere behind Cade, the snick of a match strike preceded dim flickering light on the walls.

"Okay," Max said. "So, I set your leg, built you a fire, gave you medicine, brought you home. And took care of you."

"Yeah?" Cade craned his neck. It was a cave. The ceiling was about head height, the walls about twice as wide. But an outcrop of rock hid Max and the light source. "So?"

"So I'm saying. I'm your friend. Don't freak out."

From around the outcrop, came a creature dressed in board shorts, a Coldplay T-shirt, and an unzipped hoodie. It would have been okay, if the legs coming out of the shorts weren't those of a gigantic dog, but they were, and it wasn't. The top half of the beast was roughly human, except for Max's snout which was slightly longer, and covered in fine brown fur. Cade's mind went full fight or flight. "What the— don't come any closer! I know karate! I'll... I can.... Hey, that's John's shirt. And the shorts he lost...."

"He had great taste in clothes, and music," Max replied.

"No," Cade said. "He was the worst."

Cade's eyes followed the workings of Max's slightly canid jaw, alternately hiding and revealing his massive K-9 teeth. And then Max's words filtered across Cade's brain. "Wait. What the fuck?! You're a fucking monster! Get away from me!"

Max sighed. "You're freaking out. I thought we agreed you wouldn't do that."

"I didn't agree to shit!" Cade yelled. The thing in the candlelight was a werewolf. And he was acting like... like a normal guy!

"Okay, calm down." Max patted the air at his waist.

"I'm stranded in the middle of the woods. I've got a broken leg. I've been kidnapped—"

"—rescued," Max put in.

"—*kidnapped*," Cade pushed on, "by a werewolf—"

"—*wolfman*, there's a difference—" Max talked over him.

"—who is a fucking *comedian*."

"Aw, it's kind of you to say," Max nodded.

"Is all this funny to you?!"

Max shrugged, making the candle bob. "It's about a three. Here's your bucket." The wolfman leaned down, his face coming inches from Cade.

The wolfman's caramel eyes stared into Cade's own. Their gold flecks swirling the constellations. His breath smelled of... mint? Was this mythical man-eating monster sucking on a breath mint?

Max set an empty plastic margarine tub in front of him, never breaking eye contact. "I thought you might like to piss in one of John's margarine tubs, since you always hated that he ate this crap."

Cade's mouth fell open.

"What?" Max tilted his head to one side.

"You've been watching us?"

Max rose and turned away. "And stealing John's clothes and discarded margarine tubs, obviously. Not much else to do up here. And you're the closest house. It's another ten miles to the Johnson's. But old man Johnson sits on his porch with a shotgun half the time. Too risky."

"So...." Cade's mind flashed to all the times they'd sat out naked in the summertime. All the times He and John had laid a blanket on the lawn and made love under the stars. "How long...." He stopped. Falling. Broken leg. Wolfman. With all that, the hole John left in his life hadn't had time to become a chasm, until now. "You watched us make love...."

"If you could call it that," Max said. "You made love, for sure, but from where I sat, he was just fucking you. He didn't deserve you, Cade."

"I... what? I'm in a cave peeing in a margarine tub while a werewolf rates my sex life...."

"Wolfman. Wolfman," Max corrected. "Werewolves change back and forth. I look like this all the time. Also, werewolves are like the village idiots of the supernatural world. Poor bastards. I mean, it's nice to be able to run to the corner store and get cream at six in the morning. But those poor fuckers shed IQ points like a Husky in a hothouse when they shift. I'd rather be smart."

"Don't change the subject!" Cade insisted. "You've been spying on me!"

"It's not like that," Max said. "I don't have TV out here, and the Cade and John show was the only thing on."

Cade rubbed his face in frustration and embarrassment. "Oh my God."

"Hey, are you gonna pee or not? I'm getting tired of standing with my back to you."

"I'm having the worst night," Cade muttered. He struggled to free his big uncircumcised cock from his jeans. Not an easy task laying on his side. His hand came away sticky. What the actual fuck?! Had the wolfman been messing with Cade while he was unconscious? But no. Cade would like to think that. He'd like to think the evidence of his arousal was from something other. But the truth was, Cade liked the idea of being watched. And, Cade couldn't deny the swirling crackling energy between Max and himself.

Images of the wolfman jacking off in the trees while John

fucked Cade doggy style on the lawn came unbidden. Cade's cock pulsed, further delaying the pee he desperately needed. He wondered what Max had between his legs? Man dick? Wolf cock? He was never going to pee at this rate.

"How's it going back there?" Max asked.

"Back off," Cade protested. "I've never had to pee laying on my side in a wolfman's cave before."

"At least you got the right species that time," Max mumbled.

The indignant remark was enough to pull Cade's mind from sex long enough to urinate. When he'd finished, covered the margarine tub, and tucked in his traitorous cock, Cade said, "I need to wash my hands."

"I've always admired your cleanliness," Max said, turning.

"Always?" This wasn't fair at all. He never pulled the blinds down at the house. After all, his place was miles from the nearest… anything. Why would he, except to deny the prying eyes of stray, voyeuristic wolfmen, apparently? "How long is always?"

Max squatted down in front of him to retrieve the tub of pee.

Cade's eyes fell on the bulge in Max's stolen shorts.

Max's hand reaching for the container blocked Cade's view. And instead of grabbing the plastic, Max pointed a finger toward his face. "I'm up here."

This was so weird. Cade's face burned. He'd just been ogling a wolfman, *and* been called out on it. When he dutifully lifted his eyes to Max's face, they found a bemused smile there.

If Cade's face burned before, now it was positively on fire.

"I'm just fucking with you," Max said. He spread his legs wider. "Feel free to bask in my magnificence."

"Is this a joke to you?" The words left Cade's mouth before he could stop them. Despite his indignance, his eyes fell greedily on the rather *large* bulge in Max's pants.

"Still about a three," Max said, picking up the tub. "Tell you what. After I get rid of this, we need to take a look at that cut on your head. That was nasty, and, you bled a lot. We need to clean that up. I'll bring something for your hands too."

"I...." Fuck it. Max was right. He wasn't threatening. Far from it. He was arousing, actually, as much as Cade hated to admit it. "Okay."

"Okay," Max agreed. He rose and disappeared around the rocky outcrop a few feet away.

Cade heard the wolfman's soft retreating steps long enough to deduce they were at the end of a long passage.

In the light of the candle that Max left burning on the sand, Cade studied his surroundings. He lay on a backpacking foam mat with another rolled up mat elevating his leg. The sandy floor had a fine, soft texture, and the gray stone walls had been carved smooth by some ancient underground river. At his feet, a pool of water about the size of a hot tub threw steam toward the rocky ceiling. Condensation formed on the rock and trickled down one side of the roof to a small knot of stone where it gathered and dripped back into the pool.

Sweat dripped from Cade's forehead into his hair. This cave was fucking hot. Cade still wore his parka, jeans, and winter boots with thick wool socks. He did his best to sit up without moving his broken leg. Still, the act jostled it enough to fucking *hurt*! With no way to support himself and shrug out of the heavy coat, Cade leaned far forward.

The world swam. He wobbled.

"Shit!" Max's voice behind him. Something fell. An old cooking pot and pan dropped to the sand beside Cade.

Woozy, Cade fell back.

Max caught him. "Easy, handsome."

Strong hairy arms wrapped around Cade's torso. The sweet,

clean scent of pine tar filled his nose. "I've got you. What were you trying to do?"

"I'm hot," Cade mumbled.

"Yeah, y' are," Max whispered. "Would you like help taking your coat off?"

"Yes, please." The world spun around Cade. He relaxed into Max's arms. "I don't feel good."

"I think you've got a concussion." His voice fell. "It was stupid and dangerous for me to have given you that sedative earlier. I'm sorry."

Cade agreed. Yet, how could he be angry at the events leading up to lying in this kind creature's strong arms. Without all this, he'd be home. Lonely, and very alone. Probably staring at pictures of him and John. "S' okay," Cade said. It was... and it wasn't. These strong warm arms belonged to a fucking wolfman!

"When you're ready, lean forward again, slowly," Max whispered in a deep, husky voice, close to Cade's ear, "and we'll get you out of that jacket." A cloud of his sweet, minty breath surrounded Cade.

Cade didn't want to leave Max's arms. His love language was touch. John's wasn't. And until this moment, Cade didn't realize how starved he was for genuine connection and affection. Ironic that he'd found it in the arms of this monster. Except, maybe John was the real monster?

"Come on," Max prodded. "Let's get you cleaned up and comfortable."

Cade leaned forward and Max helped him out of the red parka. The motion made the cave spin around him.

"Can you stay like that while I clean your wound?"

Cade took a deep breath. "I think so."

"Okay. Stay still."

Cade didn't dare move, lest the world spin out of control

and make him sick. Out of the corner of his eye, Cade watched the thick muscles of Max's back and arms work as the wolfman squatted before the steaming pool at his feet and dipped the stainless steel pot, filling it. When he rose with the full vessel and turned, Cade caught a momentary glimpse of Max's bulge before the wolfman disappeared from view behind him.

Pain exploded in Cade's head when Max touched the cloth to it. "Ow! Fuck!"

"Sorry," Max said. "It's got to be done though. Can't have his handsome head get infected."

It was already infected, but not with bacteria. Somewhere along the way, Cade had become infected by Max's scent. His humor. His kindness. And infected with curiosity about the big bulge under Max's shorts.

CHAPTER

FOUR

Rest. Cade needed rest. Not this distractingly handsome wolfman bulging out his ex-boyfriend's shorts. In fact.... Yeah. This must be a dream. A hallucination from the fall. He was probably still laying at the bottom of the cliff. Yeah. And if it was a dream, if his body was lying senseless in the forest, freezing to death, then whatever happened here in the dreamworld was alright. It was like... permission. He could let himself go. Be free. Free to let this kind wolfman take care of him. And, more than anything else, Cade longed for that. John never really did. John wasn't a nurturing soul.

"Ow!" The pain from Max's dabbing cloth on the back of his head made Cade question his concussion hallucination hypothesis.

"Sorry."

His eyes fell on the discarded parka, the drying blood showed dark maroon against the puffy red fabric. "I think my jacket is ruined."

"Sucks," Max agreed. "And where's my basket of goodies?"

Cade frowned. "What... wait? Did you just make a Red Riding Hood joke?"

"Yup."

Cade shook his head… and wished he hadn't. The world fishtailed crazily.

"Hold still, damn it, Red. I'm almost done."

"Red?" Cade frowned.

"Too soon?"

"No." Cade had to admit, he was charmed. Charmed by a wolfman. Christ, it sounded like a bad porno.

"There. No stitches. Just maybe take it easy. I'd hate to have to shave your head."

The gentle touch of Max's fingers on the back of his neck… did things for Cade. Things he'd rather a wolfman's touch not do. Traitorous body. But his body was reacting not just to the physicality, but, more the vibe.

"You got a lot of blood down your shirt," Max said. "We should take that off too, so I can wash your back."

This tickled Cade's brain as dangerous. Maybe this wolfman was just undressing him so it would be easier to eat him? No, that was stupid. Why would he clean Cade's head wound then?

Cade lifted his arms to take off his shirt, then dropped them to steady himself as the world spun.

And Max was there. Catching Cade, and wrapping a furry muscled arm around him. "I got you," Max whispered in his ear. "I got you."

A lump rose in Cade's throat. He hadn't felt this supported in years. Physically or spiritually. It just *had* to be a wolfman. Unbelievable.

Max nuzzled Cade's neck.

Cade shivered.

"Let me help," Max said. And while holding Cade, slipped him one arm at a time out of his shirt.

"I have a concussion," Cade said. "You're taking advantage of me."

"I'm grooming you," Max said.

"I don't think you know what that means in the modern political context."

In answer, Max licked Cade's ear.

"Well," Cade gave a tiny cough, "maybe... you do."

A cloth of warm water traced its way down Cade's back.

Max still had an arm around Cade, and now the hand on his chest sought out his nipple and gave it a quick strum.

Cade bit his lip. His balls tingled. A fresh pulse of excitement swelled his cock.

The cloth traced between Cade's shoulder blades and down. And again. All the way down. Water streamed down him, soaking his robin's egg blue, micro model, expensive, underwear. "Hey! You're soaking my pants."

"Oh dear," Max said, "Whatever should we *do*? I guess your pants will have to come off, then."

"I'm fine wet," Cade crossed his arms.

"Yes, you are," Max said.

This was on the edge of bullshit. "Can I have my shirt back?"

"Let me wash it," Max said. "Are you cold?"

"No," Cade admitted.

"No shirt, no shoes, *full* service," Max said.

Cade wished the wolfman was in front of him so he could see Max's facial expression.

Max traced complicated patterns on Cade's back with his fingertips. He leaned in and whispered, "you can't just sit there in wet pants all night."

"You want to take my pants off, and you haven't even kissed me?" Cade meant it as a joke. But before he could clarify, or even react, the wolfman was in front of him, straddling him.

Max laid Cade back, gently supporting him. The wolfman turned Cade's head so his cut wouldn't be on the mat, tilting his chin up and bringing their eyes in line.

Musky, male scent mixed with pine tar and mint filled Cade's nose. He couldn't think. Max's intense caramel gaze held Cade under its spell. The lust swirling in the wolfman's eyes traveled through the air, entering Cade's body as he lay helplessly pinned under the beast.

Blood rushed to Cade's cock. It grew and thickened in his jeans, making them tight and uncomfortable. Cade wiggled his hips unconsciously, trying to ease the discomfort in his crotch.

"What are you doing down there?" Max asked, his voice somewhere between a whisper and a growl. He pressed the enormous bulge in his shorts against Cade's belly.

Minty breath puffed across Cade's cheek and tickled his ear. "I...." Goddamn it he couldn't think with the sexy wolfman bearing down on him. "These pants are wet and uncomfortable."

The corners of Max's mouth curled up, exposing his pearly oversized canines. "Sorry, not sorry," he said wolfishly.

And that husky, growling voice brought Cade's cock to full attention, making his jeans a horrible prison. He shifted his hips, trying to get some relief.

"What do you want?" Max asked. He nuzzled Cade's cheek, running the soft fur of his snout along Cade's jaw and gave Cade's ear a tentative lick.

Goddamn it. How long had this sex monster been watching him? Did Max know that Cade's ears were his magic button? And fuck all that, Max knew what Cade wanted. Why was he tormenting him? Cade shifted his hips again.

"Not good enough," Max whispered. "Use your words." Again, Max bore down on Cade. The thick shaft and bulbus knot at the base of Max's cock pressed into Cade's belly through the thin fabric.

It wasn't fair. Cade couldn't be expected to think rationally under these conditions. He had no idea how long it had been since John made love to him, or even, how long it had been since he made love to himself. Quick lackluster jerks in the shower didn't count.

Max stared down at Cade expectantly.

"I...." Fuck it. "I want you to take my pants off."

Max smiled like he'd won something. "I thought you wanted a kiss first?" Again, the wolfman pressed his monstrous virility into the soft flesh of Cade's stomach.

"Kiss me, then," Cade said.

Max brought his lips so close to Cade's that Cade could feel the fur at their delicious edge. "Where are your manners? You're in my home. I rescued you. I took care of you. Don't you think you owe me deference?"

"Please," Cade swallowed, "kiss me."

And then, Max did. His broad, wide tongue brushed across Cade's lips before pushing inside Cade's mouth.

When their tongues met, something inside Cade snapped. He brought his arms up and buried his fingers in the soft fur on the back of Max's neck, pulling his sexy lover closer. The pain in his head, and the pain in his leg vanished behind the flush of arousal.

Max pushed his cock harder into Cade's belly, making it difficult to breathe.

Cade's pants squeezed his swollen shaft so hard he thought he might burst the button if Max didn't free him soon.

And still, the wolfman's tongue probed and pressed Cade's eager mouth. Max's breath rushed inside Cade, filling his lungs with minty pulmonary ejaculate. Cade wanted it. He wanted Max to fill him in every way there was, in every hole he had.

As if Max could hear Cade's thoughts, he put a hand between them and tugged the elastic waistband of his board shorts down past his monstrous erection. The wolfman's cock hit Cade's belly with a wet slap. A thin string of pre-cum flew from the tip and landed between Cade's toned solar plexus. Max pulled his mouth away and met Cade's eyes. "You're so handsome. You've got me so, so hard...."

"Yeah," was all Cade could manage. He shifted his hips again. Max was supposed to take *Cade's* pants off. Free *Cade's* cock. Not his own, damn it.

Max took Cade's chin in his soft, furry hand. "I don't want to fuck you. I—"

Cade opened his mouth to protest, but the wolfman put a finger to his lips.

"Shh." Max hissed. "I started watching you and John out of boredom. And then, out of horniness. But, after a while... things changed. I saw how he treated you. I could sense your sadness, through the walls of your house and the glass in your windows. I watched, longing for your kindness. Vowing I would always honor your vulnerable heart if you entrusted it to me. So, I'm saying, I don't want to *fuck* you. I want to make *love* to you. I want to honor your tender heart and your sexy body. I want to fill you with my love. And... I want your forgiveness for invading your privacy."

Cade wished the woke wolfman would shut up and fuck him. He shifted under Max, trying to lift his hips without putting pressure on his injured leg. "Please...."

"Say it," Max nuzzled Cade's face. "I've dreamed about it. I've cum thinking about it. Ask me to make love to you."

Jesus. If that's what it took to get at that monster meat, so be it. "Make love to me," Cade moaned, squirming and sliding against the thick cock oozing arousal on his belly.

Max gripped his chin, forcing their eyes to meet. "Say it again."

Goddammit! "Make love to me, Max!" He pushed his hips up. Pain shot through him. Best not to try that again.

"Yes!" Max thrust his hips, sliding the tapered head of his

penis into the shallow gully between Cade's pecks before climbing off.

Cade released the fur on the back of Max's neck with a plaintive whimper.

"I'm right here," the wolfman cooed. "Just got to get you out of these clothes without hurting you."

Cade thought the task impossible. Max had splinted his broken leg over his jeans. But the wolfman extended his hind leg and dexterously cut the pant leg in a wide circle just above the splint. Max's razor sharp claw severed the fabric as easily as the sharpest pair of shears. Then, Max stretched that same leg severing the outside seam right up to Cade's waist. And somehow, Max made the whole operation sexy, drawing his claw along the denim, and just barely touching the skin underneath.

The unspoken danger of Max's sharp claws made Cade painfully hard. He moaned as the wolfman did the same to his designer briefs, slicing the soft cloth along Cade's hip, then flipping the fabric aside, leaving Cade's dick pulsing and lonely in the humid subterranean air.

Cade moaned and squeezed his muscles, lifting his cock off his belly, then releasing and letting it slap down into the happy trail of soft hair.

"Patience, love," Max whispered as he ran a sharp fingernail lightly along the length of Cade's cock, tickling on the edge of pain. Scratching Cade's desperate itch without satisfying it. He removed the remnants of Cade's clothes the same way, cutting them in half without moving Cade a centimeter. Max flung the useless fabric aside, leaving Cade naked, exposed, and helpless under the wolfman's lusty gaze. "I've dreamed of this moment for so long..." he whispered.

Max slipped out of his clothes in a supernaturally fast blur Cade couldn't follow. Then, he straddled Cade, bringing his cock alongside Cade's own.

Cade whimpered, wanting more. Wanting the wolfman to take him. Ravage him. Fuck him hard.

A soft growl escaped Max. The sexy mythical beast leaned down, placing his elbows on either side of Cade's head, pressing their bodies and cocks together, trapped in the soft fur of Max's groin and belly. He sent his velveteen tongue tracing the curve behind Cade's ear. The wolfman moved his hips oh so slowly back and forth, sliding that monstrous canid cock against Cade's own.

The sensations on Cade's dick were delicious and maddening at the same time. Max's thick, hard, meaty cock on one side and soft fur on the other made Cade's dick spill over with passion, coating both with precum. And he couldn't respond. If he tried to raise his hips, it put pressure on the broken leg, sending excruciating pain through his body. All Cade could do was lie there and take what this kind, sexy wolfman offered.

"I love your scent," Max whispered. "It's like coming home." He tucked an errant curl of brown hair behind Cade's ear and kissed him.

Cade kissed back, raising his head and once again gripping the silky fur of Max's neck. Their tongues danced in the warm, minty breeze of Max's breath. The gusts grew more rapid as the speed of the wolfman's hips increased. Between them, their cocks danced too, sliding back and forth in impossibly slick suits of pre-cum.

When he couldn't stand it any longer, Cade broke the kiss. "Please, fuck me!"

Max nuzzled Cade's cheek, then pulled back and met his eyes. "The things I want to do to you, I can't do with your leg broken."

"Wait, no!" No way was this sexy, supernatural cock tease was going to leave him hard and longing until his leg healed!

Max put a finger to his lips. "This isn't the last time we'll be together... unless you want it to be."

That wasn't even what Cade had been thinking. He just wanted to cum, feeling adored and connected in a way he hadn't in, maybe... ever? "Max," he whined. "Please...."

Max reached between them and pressed their cocks together, circling them both at once in his meaty hand. "Please what?" He grinned, showing his huge, pointed, perfect teeth.

Cade couldn't. He'd lost the power of speech. His mind formed the words *stroke us*, but his mouth only managed to say, "ugh, mmm."

Apparently, Max spoke Cade's lust language. He slid his hand up their cocks, squeezing, and then sliding slowly back to their roots, and squeezing again. Max's wetness dripped down onto Cade's dick, further coating it. Cade couldn't ever remember being this hard for anyone else, not even himself. His sex was an iron rod, and Max an expert smith.

Cade kept trying to pump his hips, only to be interrupted by the blinding pain in his leg. Yet, somehow, the juxtaposition of sensations intensified the pleasure.

Max quickened his pace, sliding and squeezing their cocks together. Max's bigger and differently shaped dick sent plenty of all natural wolfman lube onto Cade's straining cock.

A bulge grew at the base of Max's veiny red shaft, bumping against Cade's balls as Max's furry hips pumped faster. "I've wanted you for so long." The word's left Max's lips between barely audible growls. "You're so handsome. So Kind." Max's hips became a blur.

Cade stroked the fine fur on Max's back as the sexy monster above him pistoned his cock against Cade's. "Please," Cade begged, "cum for me. Come all over me! Cover me in cum!"

That was all Max needed. The big wolfman cock pulsed against Cade's. Spurt after spurt of hot thick spend burst between them, soaking and warming them, dripping down Cade's sides.

The heat, the cum, the delicious slickness, and the weight of this soft, sexy, muscled creature above him sent Cade over the edge. His dick surged against the wolfman's. "Yes, oh fuck," he groaned, adding his spurting spunk to the growing rivers of cream cascading between the two lovers and spilling over onto the mat.

Cade bucked against Max. And Max rocked him off the mat just far enough to slip his strong, heavily muscled arms all the way around Cade, holding him so very tight as their orgasms subsided.

Max collapsed on top of Cade. The thick mane of fur on the wolfman's neck tickled Cade's cheek. He slid a large hand up Cade's spine to cradle his skull. And then, slowly, Max started dragging them toward the dripping, steaming pool at their feet.

"What?" Cade whispered.

"Best cleanup, ever," Max said. "Right into the hot spring. We'll have to keep your leg out of the water. Heat's not good for it." While he spoke, Max used his strong haunches to spin them around. The dexterous creature somehow managed to keep Cade on the mat. They ended up heads pointing toward the water.

"Okay," Max said. "Here we go." He climbed off Cade then. Strings of their combined spend dripped lewdly back onto Cade's belly.

Splashing behind him told Cade that Max had entered the pool. Big hands gripped Cade under his armpits and slid him off the foam mat and into the steaming water.

True to his word, Max stopped when Cade's knees were at the edge. His strong arms came around Cade, stroking his stomach and sides clean while Cade's head rested on Max's chest. The wolfman slid further behind Cade, bringing his head to Max's shoulder. "Hi lover," he said.

"Hi." Cade reached a hand back and stroked the wolfman's neck. The water's heat sent pins and needles along Cade's skin, so hot Cade could barely stand it. With the passion between his legs sated, the rest of Cade's body let him know the abuse he'd suffered over the last few hours *hurt*. "I wasn't really in pain, until now."

"I'm sorry, sexy man," Max said. "I'll get us cleaned up, then I'll take you home."

"I'm going to need a hospital," Cade said.

"I know," Max agreed. "But I'll get you home and you can call an ambulance." He chuckled. "It's not like I can drive you to town."

"How did you end up out here. How... how do you know to speak English. You... you kind of seem like a regular person, but you said you look like this all the time? I don't get it?"

"Shhh, honey," Max whispered. "All in due time. Just enjoy the moment."

Cade did. He enjoyed Max's strong hands, stroking him and cleaning the product of their savage coupling from Cade's abused skin. He enjoyed lying back on Max's chest, the wolfman's hard muscle covered in soft fur. He enjoyed letting go all control. Cade was a helpless victim in the clutches of a savage monster. Injured and alone in the world. He had nowhere to be. Nothing to do. He could just be, lying in the arms of someone who adored him. The release of expectation and the demands of the outside world was just what Cade needed.

They stayed like that for a long time. Long after their bodies were clean, and the meager current of the underground hot spring washed away any evidence of their debauchery, Cade lay in Max's arms.

"I don't ever want to move again."

"Why?" Max asked.

"Well," Cade ran a hand down Max's haunch underwater, "I've got a strong sexy wolfman holding me tight. But also, when I move, it's going to hurt."

"We should go, soon," Max said. "I've been selfish. You need medical attention."

"I don't want to go," Cade said. He did actually, really, want to go to the hospital. What he *didn't* want was to say goodbye to Max. He had this feeling that the wolfman would disappear in the daylight. That this whole thing was some kind of fever dream. What if he woke to find he was still at the bottom of a cliff with a concussion and a broken leg, and there never was a sexy wolfman named Max?

"Dude," Max said, "don't be an ass. You need a doctor." He pulled Cade from the water, sliding him deftly onto the mat, keeping him out of the sand. Then, the wolfman produced a towel from elsewhere in the cave. Starting at Cade's feet, Max patted him dry, and kissed the fresh skin in the towel's wake. By the time Max finished, Cade's cock bobbed against his stomach, hard and aching for more of his lover's touch.

CHAPTER
FIVE

Max wrapped Cade in a blanket, ignoring his throbbing erection. "It's a long walk back to your house," he said, picking Cade up, like one might pick up a puppy.

"You're going to carry me the whole way?"

Max nodded. "So," his eyes met Cade's, and his voice held a note of apology, "I'll need to cover your head. It's not that I don't trust you, it's just... well, I've got a good thing here, and, I've been burned before."

"I would never...." Cade trailed off. Every bad guy *ever* probably said that. "Okay," he relented. It sucked too, because he really wanted a tour of the cave. Clearly, there was a lot more to it than this little room with the hot spring.

Max draped the blanket over Cade's face, held him close, and strode toward the front of the cave.

When they hit the outside air, Cade was grateful for the hood. The cold seeped in through the blanket. And the walk fucking hurt. Cade's broken leg bounced with each step, though he could tell Max was trying to be careful. "Please," Cade said, "distract me. Tell me things. Are there a lot of... people like you?

How do you speak English so well and understand, like, society?"

"Do you want your hood off now?" Max asked.

"Yeah," Cade said. "And stop — Ow! — changing the subject."

"Okay," Max said, "I'll humor you."

"All I know are these woods and the surrounding houses. My first memories are of a kindly old man. I used to sleep in his basement. And he would feed me at night. Read me stories...." The wolfman trailed off.

Cade sensed a wound there, and didn't probe.

Max shook himself. "The Appalachian Trail is up there." Max inclined his head in the direction of the distant mountains. "Sometimes, I can go talk to the hikers. Once in a while, I get lucky. One guy even gave me his phone. Said he didn't want contact with the world anymore."

Max looked at Cade for a response.

Cade had nothing. He felt sort of hurt that he wasn't Max's first human tryst. And jealous that Max was off hooking up with random hikers instead of pining away for Cade in the woods behind Cade's house. It was stupid.

When Cade didn't say anything, Max kept going. "I find stuff too. Stuff that falls out of people's packs, or that's too heavy and they don't want to carry it anymore. So yeah, I do alright.

"Wait, wait, wait, Cade said, struggling to sit up a little taller in Max's arms. "You have a cell phone?"

"Had," Max said. "No one to pay the bill. We're here."

IT WAS STRANGE FOR CADE, watching the wolfman pacing about his house, fussing over him, getting him pillows and blankets, making hot coffee (Cade explained each step from the couch).

After they called the ambulance, Max waited with Cade.

Cade squeezed Max's soft furry hand. "So, will I see you again?"

"Count on it." Max squeezed back. "I am going to make love to you all night long. When you get back."

When the sound of crunching tires came from outside, Max leaned down and kissed Cade, their tongues doing a dance Cade hoped to repeat every day for the rest of his life. Except tomorrow. Tomorrow he'd be in the hospital. Not exactly wolfman territory.

"Stay here," Cade said. "I have a laptop. We can video chat."

"I *like* my place," Max said.

IT ENDED up being three days, actually. And by the time the rideshare dropped him off at home with a cast and a pair of crutches, Cade was ready for his own bed, and his own food. And as it turned out, his food was ready for him.

The delicious smells of sautéed vegetables and cooking meat greeted Cade when he opened the front door, teetering awkwardly on his crutches.

"Oh, Hey!" Max called from the kitchen. He was dressed in a pair of Cade's cutoff jeans, and nothing else, holding a spatula.

The wolfman's muscles bunched and stretched deliciously, as he set the spatula down, walked up to Cade, and stood awkwardly staring at Cade's crutches. "How can I help you?"

Conflicting emotions tumbled over each other in Cade's mind. He was thrilled to see his wolfman again. But Max had seemingly made himself at home in his absence, and he felt a little violated. Still, Cade had invited him to stay before he'd left, and Max had declined. How long had Max been in the house? Had he gone through Cade's things?

"Cade?"

Just for a moment, the foreignness of the wolfman's face shocked Cade. The otherness.

Max's face fell. He'd seen it in Cade's eyes. "I'm sorry," he said, turning for the door. "I shouldn't have come."

Cade's stomach opened into a huge pit. He tottered on his crutches, unsure how to chase his erstwhile lover. "Wait!"

Max stopped, hand on the back door handle.

"Don't go."

The wolfman turned and crossed his arms over his chest, looking at the floor.

"I...." Cade couldn't seem to gather his thoughts. "I just wasn't expecting you to be here. You said you preferred your own place."

"I couldn't wait," Max said. "I kept going back and forth, checking to see if you were back yet. One day turned into two.... I was worried, okay? What if there was something wrong we didn't know about? That was a big fall. It was stupid of me to wait to get you help. I took advantage of you."

"Max, I...."

"What if you had internal bleeding? What if I killed you? And the three days. I was scared, Cade." He sniffed through his big wide snout. "Plus, your food was going to go bad. I had nothing else to do, so I started cooking...."

Cade still didn't know what the fuck to feel. He felt all the things. But he couldn't let Max stand by the door with his head drooping.

"Could I have a hug?"

Max raised his head.

Cade bit his lip, and nodded. He was in Max's thick arms almost before he saw the wolfman move.

Max lifted Cade off his feet and spun him around as the crutches clattered to the floor.

"Okay, okay," Cade laughed. "I'm still pretty banged up."

"Oh." Max stopped spinning and held still. "Sorry," he said, chastened.

"Kiss me," Cade said.

Their lips met, and then their tongues. Cade traced the sharp tips of Max's fangs. A thrill shivered through him. The love mixed with danger tingled down his spine and settled in his balls.

An acrid smell met Cade's nose. "Something's burning."

"Shit! The stir-fry!" Without putting Cade down, Max walked them into the kitchen. He held Cade one-handed while taking the pan off the stove and turning off the burner. "Should still be okay," he said in Cade's ear. "It'll need to cool. It's too hot to eat."

"I'm not," Cade whispered.

Max growled low in his throat.

The sound-waves sent blood to Cade's groin. He held Max tighter and nuzzled into the soft fur of the wolfman's neck. When he opened his eyes, they met the empty place on the wall where John's artwork used to hang. And then the place where John's chair used to be. A wave of loss washed over him. "Make love to me."

Max kissed him, and carried him to the bedroom. Then, with Cade lying on the bed, Max carefully slid Cade's loose sweatpants down over his legs, careful not to snag them on the gleaming white plaster cast.

Cade reached out.

Max straddled him, as he'd done in the cave. His cock bulged in his tight shorts.

"That looks uncomfortable," Cade said, reaching for the button.

"You too," Max said, staring down at the erection straining the soft bamboo of Cade's briefs.

93

Max slid the blue fabric down just under Cade's balls. His throbbing shaft fell back against Cade's hairy belly with a smack and a string of pre-cum.

Likewise, Cade popped the button on the wolfman's shorts and pulled the zipper down, reveling in the sight of Max's huge, red, pulsing cock. The vision made him shiver. He licked his lips, remembering the salty-sweet musk of the wolfman's cock. A taste he wanted again. He wrapped his hand around the shaft. Moisture oozed from Max's tip, and Cade rubbed his palm over the spot. Lubed now, Cade slid his hand down Max's long shaft, bumping the growing knot at its base.

"Oh, you dirty boy," Max groaned. "I want to taste you."

"Me too," Cade sighed, unable to take his eyes off the glistening prize between Max's legs.

Max climbed off Cade, slid the useless shorts down his hairy haunches, and kicked them across the room. Then, the wolfman straddled Cade's face, the paws of his hind legs pinning Cade's head in place. He gripped Cade's head and tilted it back, bumping the angled head of his beastly cock against Cade's lips. "Open up, pup," he grunted.

Cade did, wishing he could unhinge his jaw to take Max's big dick down his throat. With the wolfman's thick furry haunches encasing him from head to elbow, Cade could do nothing but suck. Max had Cade's arms pinned at his sides.

Soft fur tickled Cade's cheeks as the wolfman rocked his hips slowly, further and further each time until Cade's throat opened and Max's angry knot bumped against Cade's lips. With each gentle thrust, Max pulled back so Cade could take a breath before sheathing his cock once again in Cade's hungry mouth. The salty taste of the wolfman's cock and the musky smell of the fur around Max's groin drove Cade wild. His neglected dick bounced plaintively against the happy trail on his belly.

And then, Max withdrew from Cade's mouth and turned

around, presenting his swelling knot and huge balls to Cade's lips. Max bent forward, taking Cade in his mouth. The wolfman eased the underside of Cade's shaft along his long, velvety tongue while gently scratching the top of his cock with those big sharp wolfman teeth. Max's balls trapped Cade's moans of ecstasy deep in his throat.

Cade worshipped at the alter of the wolfman's knot and balls, licking and sucking the salty musk while Max swallowed Cade's cock. And just when Cade thought the fist sized knot at the base of Max's staff couldn't get any bigger, the wolfman pulled away.

"I want to be inside you," Max growled.

"I want that too," Cade said, "but I don't know if I can take you."

"You can."

Max's confident alpha tones sent tingles tracing down Cade's spine. He climbed off Cade, and in one lightning fast motion, sliced Cade's underwear down the side with a sharp claw, parting the fabric and stinging Cade's hip with his barely controlled excitement.

"If you keep this up, I won't have any underwear left," Cade said.

"That'd be a real shame," Max said, in a voice that made it clear it wasn't. He gently lifted Cade's legs off the bed, resting the plaster cast on his shoulder. And then the wolfman's wet tip pressed between Cade's cheeks.

"Go slow," Cade begged.

"Shh," Max grunted. He gently bumped the tip of his shaft against Cade's opening. The wolfman rocked his hips, kissing Cade's tight ring and pulling back, over and over.

Lifetimes passed as Max teased the entrance to Cade's hole, touching his cock to the spot and pulling back, lubricating Cade with his copious pre-cum.

"Please," Cade moaned.

Max ignored him. Bumping against the edge of paradise and pulling back again and again.

"Please," Cade begged again, tugging at the fur on Max's arms.

Max chuffed and pushed a tiny bit harder. The tip of his cock finally tickled the inside of Cade's tight ring, pushing him open just a little more.

"Yes," Cade moaned, "please...." His whole body tingled. His stomach buzzed with excitement.

Max smiled down at him, then gave a long, low growl from deep in his chest. He pulled back and kept bumping gently at Cade's horny hole. Slow kisses, cock to ass.

Cade grabbed fistfuls of the hair on Max's flanks and pulled the wolfman toward his trembling treasure box. "Come on!"

And then, with a short throaty bark, Max was inside Cade. The big angled head of the wolfman's dick pushed past Cade's opening to thump against his pleasure center. "Mmm," Cade moaned, "fuck me."

Max leaned down, bringing his face to Cade's own, as he had in the cave, except this time Max's cock stretched Cade wider than he'd ever been opened before. The pain of the wolf-man's sudden penetration and enormous dick mixed with the intense pleasure of that monster cock thumping Cade's prostate with each thrust.

The delicious sensation of the wolfman's fur on Cade's chest sent tingles across his skin. Max's musky scent filled his nose as Max laid his long, soft snout along Cade's cheek.

Cade shivered as Max began alternately nipping at his neck and licking his ear. The rhythm of Max's hips increased. Something big pushed against Cade's ass.

"I'm going to knot you," Max grunted. "I'm going to fill you, and breed you, and mark you as my mate forever."

Cade wanted that. But the huge bulge knocking at his back door scared the hell out of him. "I don't know if I can take it," he whispered.

"Oh," the wolfman snarled, "you'll take it, love." And with that, the wolfman slid back, then slammed forward.

"Oh, God," Cade moaned when the knot bumped up against him. "No!"

"You want me to stop?" Max asked.

Cade did... and he didn't.

"You want me to pull out and leave you empty?"

"Please, no. I want you."

"Then, take it!" Again, Max pulled back, then jammed his hips forward.

Cade moaned in fear and pleasure mixed. His cock shuddered into Max's belly fur with each thrust of the wolfman's powerful hips.

"Come on," Max growled. "Be a good boy and take my big knot." He punctuated this with another strong thrusting attack on Cade's ass.

Cade tried to relax. He let out a breath. And on Max's next thrust, Cade felt himself open, taking the knot halfway before squeezing it out.

"Show me you want me, Cade. Take it!"

Max's gruff voice and commanding words thrilled Cade. He wanted to be owned, marked, knotted, and mated. And on Max's next thrust, the big round knot of his cock forced its way into Cade's tight, hungry ass.

"Oh, ow, holy fuck!" Cade gasped. The sharp pain shocked him. Driving him into a state of hypersensitivity. He'd never felt so alive, so present with a lover.

"Good boy," Max growled. His canid haunches blurred. His knot banged on the inside of Cade's ass, as if it wanted to get out.

But there *was* no out. They were knotted. Young, handsome human and wolfman joined by cock and locked by the knot. Max reared up. He looked down at Cade with smoldering caramel eyes. His hand circled Cade's hard, aching dick.

"Yes," Cade moaned. "Fuck me!"

Max pumped into Cade with feral fury. "Take my love," he growled. "Take my dick!" He dropped Cade's cock and grabbed Cade's hips, plunging in deep, deep inside. His heavy balls slapped Cade's ass in a driving rhythm.

"Fuck!" Cade grunted. As Max plowed into him, Cade's cock slapped his chest. "Oh, yes," he moaned as his dick spurted thick jets of cum. He couldn't let go of Max's fur for fear the wolfman would drive him off the bed in his passion. He could only watch as his cock rained cum across his chest in fiery hot drops.

Max plunged into Cade and held him hard against his pulsing cock. "Painting your insides...." He growled.

Cade trembled as the wolfman's gigantic cock throbbed inside him, spilling his spend. Marking Cade. Making him the wolfman's mate.

Max collapsed on top of Cade, planting his elbows on either side of his head.

Cade wrapped his arms around Max's back, relishing the soft fur over hard muscle. "That was... unexpected."

"What part of it was unexpected?" Max asked between licks and nibbles on Cade's ear.

"Well, I thought it was going to be sweet, tender tantric love. You know our first—"

"Yeah, uh, dude. For sure, I'm deeply smitten, but... um..." Max sat up and motioned to himself "*wolfman.*"

"Well, *wolfman,*" Cade grinned, "that was amazing."

"Yeah," Max looked down. "Sorry about the ruined orgasm."

Cade reached out and gave Max's chest a loving stroke. "You owe me one." Then, "also, it was kind of hot."

Max looked up. "Yeah?"

Cade trailed a finger along the velvety fur between his lover's pecks. "Yeah."

Max started to roll off, but inadvertently dragged Cade with him. "Yeah, so, I want to lie beside you, but um..." He cast his eyes down.

"Is this what they mean by tying the knot?" Cade grinned.

"Oh, gee. Never heard that one before." Max jerked his hips back, bumping his bulge against the inside of Cade's hole.

"Ok, ok!" Cade grabbed Max's shoulders. "Brat!" He pulled Max down to kiss him.

Max broke the kiss and grinned. "Takes one to know one."

Again, Cade pulled the wolfman's mouth to his. Soft flesh on flesh, seeking every sensation.

"Keep that up, and we'll be stuck together all day," Max said.

Cade gazed into Max's caramel, golden flecked eyes. "Would that be so bad?"

"No," Max said.

They made love again. This time more slowly, gently. Eyes locked in their moment of ecstasy, soul to soul. And when they finally finished, Cade fell asleep with his kind, handsome, wolfish lover still deep inside him.

VAMPIRE MOTORCYCLE GANGED

CHAPTER
ONE

The slap stung Jesse to his core. He was used to the hot tingling pain on his cheek. Sometimes he invited it. The pain woke him up inside, made everything more real. Hell, sometimes he deliberately acted like a brat so Tom would slap him. But not this time. This wasn't play. They weren't doing a scene. They were making one. Right in the middle of the Cheers Queers dance floor.

"Fuck you!" Jesse shouted, trying to make himself heard above the pulsing beat.

Tom's lower jaw practically unhinged in shock. His slate-gray eyes narrowed. His nostrils flared.

Jesse didn't wait around for Tom to wind up again. He slipped behind the smooth-chested Adonis dancing with them and weaved his way off the dance floor, hoping to get out of the club's front doors before Tom caught his elbow. He burst through the double doors into the scorching Vegas heat. Even at midnight, the temperature hadn't dipped much below one hundred. The arid desert air dried the sweat from Jesse's buff body, cooling him even in the inferno.

Not wanting to hang around out front for Tom to find, Jesse

headed for the parking lot. He checked behind him as he turned the corner — and bumped into someone.

Something cracked his shin.

Arms came around him. "Whoa!"

"Sorry!" Jesse struggled to right himself.

The arms easing Jesse to his feet belonged to the most handsome man he'd ever laid eyes on. Handsome was leaning on a massive black motorcycle, smoking a clove cigarette.

"I don't think you're supposed to park here," Jesse said, and immediately wanted to die. What a fucking idiot.

Handsome smiled without parting his lips. "I'm not worried about it," he said. He looked Jesse up and down. "You're bleeding."

Jesse raised a hand to his face, thinking Tom had cut him with his ring.

Handsome let out a plume of smoke that turned pink in the parking lot's sodium vapor lights. "No. Your leg. Must have caught it on the foot peg." He gestured with his cigarette to the back of the bike.

"Um, yeah." Jesse hoped eventually he'd stop sounding like a moron. He checked over his shoulder again.

Handsome raised an eyebrow. "Expecting someone?" He fixed Jesse with an appraising gaze from white irises that didn't match his dark hair.

"I..." Those eyes. Something in them laid Jesse bare. As if Handsome could see into his soul. And then there was the rest of the guy. Slim without being skinny. Toned without being muscly. Short dark hair, gray just kissing his temples. He wore a leather vest with nothing underneath. His defined pecs showed the faintest traces of hair that thickened in the center and formed a happy trail leading to the button of stretch jeans that hugged every curve of a big, circumcised cock. Jesse's eyes came to rest there and didn't move.

"You know you stopped talking, right?"

"Huh? Oh. Yeah." He tore his eyes away from the outline of the handsome biker's dick long enough to check over his shoulder again.

"Escaping a bad date?" Handsome asked.

Their eyes met again. God damn, those eyes. "Something like that."

"Need a ride out of here?"

"On that?" Jesse squeaked. He wished for death.

The guy flashed him a mischievous, closed-mouth smile. "Yup."

Jesse didn't need a ride. He'd have to ride home with Tom, or, well, things would... escalate. Except, right now, his face stung. And he was so sick and tired of walking on eggshells, never knowing what would set Tom off. Well, riding home on the back of this handsome stranger's motorcycle would definitely set Tom off, so fuck it. "Yeah."

"Alright." Handsome crushed his cigarette into the pavement with the square toe of his engineer boot. "Hop on," he said, reaching for the glasses case between his handlebars.

Jesse looked for helmets hanging on the bike somewhere, but there were none. Nor were there places to put them. He opened his mouth to say something, but saw the handsome biker slip sunglasses over his face. *Sunglasses. At midnight. On a motorcycle. With no helmet!* Jesse took a step back.

"What?" Handsome asked.

The crack of the club's metal door banging open echoed off the buildings across the street.

"Jesse!" Tom shouted.

"Nothing," Jesse said. "Let's go!" He climbed on the bike.

The machine roared to life, drowning out anything else Tom might be yelling.

It felt *so* fucking good, defying Tom. Controlling his destiny again, even if that control lasted just long enough to give it to this nameless biker. He was wild and free!

"Hold on tight!" Handsome said. He gunned the engine. They roared out of the parking lot. The biker leaned in hard, turning them onto the street, riding back across the front of the club.

Tom stood tracking them with an angry glare, open-mouthed.

On impulse, Jesse extended his arm and flipped Tom off. He'd pay for that later. But right now, Jesse was queen of the world, riding bitch on this handsome hunk's bike. He wrapped his arms tight around the man and let his hands rest on the hard muscle of the biker's chest.

The night sped by in flashes of light streaked by tears from Jesse's wind-watery eyes. And then they were on the strip. The neon rainbow streaked by, leaving bright contrails in the desert darkness as they sped dangerously fast *between* the lanes of cars.

The breeze dried the remaining sweat from dancing, leaving Jesse cold in the hot night. He snuggled into Handsome, pressing his cock into the small of Handsome's back.

At a traffic light, stopped in front of some gaudy neon monolithic casino, Jesse asked, "Don't you want to know where I live?"

"Not especially," Handsome said.

His words hit Jesse like a fist. Jesse's heart pounded. "Then where are we going?"

"When was the last time you felt this alive? This free?" Handsome asked.

Jesse asked himself the same question. "Never."

"Then, does it matter?"

"I guess not." Jesse said.

"Then buckle up. It's going to be a wild night."

Before Jesse could mention the fact that there were no seatbelts, the light turned green and the bike whisked them around the corner, and into the black. He'd meant to ask Handsome for his name at the traffic light but was so addled by the revelation that Handsome wasn't actually taking him home, he'd forgotten.

They merged onto the freeway. The midnight desert heat blasted them as if there were a truck driving in front of them with a giant hair dryer pointed out of the back. They rocketed past all the traffic on the Fifteen. The sweltering night pushed him back, forcing him to lock his arms around the dark, dangerous stranger and press his body into the leather on the man's back. An electric tingle ran through Jesse. His fingers were jumper cables of desire, and this sexy stranger, a battery of lust, charging Jesse. All this motorcycle wielding stranger had to do was turn the key.

Though it scared him to get closer to the pavement at this speed, Jesse allowed himself to lean into the turn with this stranger. The danger aroused him almost as much as the hard muscle under his fingers. They corkscrewed around the exit's turns and rocketed through a red light onto Charleston Boulevard.

"Fuck!" Jesse yelled, "you're going to get us killed!"

In answer, the stranger just laughed.

Jesse's fingers clenched around the flesh of the stranger's abs. His heart hammered in his chest, fighting to break his ribs and escape to safety.

Ahead, a green arrow flicked on just in time for them to lean so far over, Jesse's knee nearly grazed the rushing asphalt. The rider dodged and weaved through the cars and crowds of First Friday in the Arts District. The artists, freaks, and wannabes shook their fists as the roaring motorcycle made its way down the street.

Jesse mumbled half-forgotten childhood prayers to a god he didn't believe in.

At impossible speed, the stranger leaned again and sent the bike rocketing through the half-shattered door of an abandoned warehouse. Inside, the biker jammed on the brakes and sent the bike into a wild fishtailing circle, rubber and smoke squealing loud in the empty warehouse's dark echoing corners.

TWO

When they'd stopped, Jesse leaped from the bike. "What the actual fuck!" he shouted, fists clenched at his sides. "I lost count of the number of times you almost got us killed! I'm fucking out of here!"

Jesse made it two steps toward the door before the man appeared in front of him. *Appeared!* The man hadn't run. Hadn't walked into Jesse's path. One second, the way was clear. The next, the man was in front of him, grabbing his chin.

"Zero," he said, fixing Jesse with those enchanting white irises.

"Huh?" It didn't occur to Jesse to struggle. He had no thought of pushing the man away. In that moment, he wanted only to stand, feeling somehow naked and helpless in the man's intense gaze.

"The number of times I almost got us killed. Zero."

And then his lips were on Jesse's. His cool tongue forcing Jesse's lips apart, spreading him.

No. No. This nameless man had almost killed him! Jesse put his hands on Handsome's chest to push him away. And then his tongue found the fangs. Jesse traced their sharp, curved shape with his tongue. Handsome had fangs!

The man grabbed a fistful of Jesse's hair, holding him in place.

Jesse pushed on the man's chest, fear rising up inside him. Fangs. What the fuck!

The biker's other arm came around Jesse, holding him in an impossibly strong iron embrace, trapping Jesse's hands between them. He pulled his lips away. "Don't pretend. I can feel your hard-on pushing into my leg. You want this."

"No, I—"

"Shut up." This time the biker smiled wide, showing his pointed teeth.

And then Jesse was being kissed again. The guy must be some kind of vampire cosplayer or something. Must be it. Still, guys like that could be dangerous… if they took things too far.

The biker's tongue forced its way into Jesse's compliant mouth.

Jesse's cock strained against the elastic waistband of his booty shorts. He leaned in, trying to get a little pressure from the biker's denim clad leg.

The biker yanked him back by his hair. "No." He stepped back, still grasping a handful of Jesse's curls. "Feel." He took Jesse's hand in his and pressed it to the huge throbbing erection in his jeans.

"Oh," Jesse gasped. He should go. Should run. Should escape into the night. But he could do none of those things, transfixed as he was by the biker's beautiful white irises, soft lips, and hard cock. The fangs, though. What did it mean?

And then the handsome biker yanked Jesse's hair, pulling him close again. The stranger jerked Jesse's head to the side, bringing his cold lips to the hot skin of Jesse's neck. The stubble on the handsome biker's chin scraped along the nape of Jesse's neck. The sensation sparked a cable of desire that ran straight to Jesse's throbbing shaft. Sharp points scratched the delicate skin of Jesse's throat.

Jesse shivered.

The points pressed.

Jesse thrust his hips, grinding his cock on the stranger's muscular thigh.

And then, stabbing. Puncturing. The pain from the stranger plunging his teeth into Jesse's jugular made his dick throb. Pleasure and pain came together in a symphony of desire. The sound of the handsome biker swallowing brought Jesse's tongue to his lips, searching for traces of the stranger's taste. His cock pulsed and begged for release from Jesse's shorts. He tried to move a hand down, but the stranger only held him tighter. All he could do was push his hips forward, crushing his needy cock against the stranger's leg.

"Please," he moaned. So thick was the fog of sexual urgency, Jesse had no idea what he begged for, he just needed something, anything. The pulling at his neck filled him with waves of delicious arousal, as if somehow having his blood drawn away left Jesse with only raw sexual desire.

His hips moved of their own accord, thrusting and grinding his cock into the fabric of his shorts, pressing himself into the hard denim-clad muscle of the vampire's thigh.

And then the vampire moaned into his neck and pulled back. Blood dripped from his luscious lips. "You taste so, so sweet, pet," he whispered. And then his lips were on Jesse again.

The coppery taste of his own blood acted as a forbidden aphrodisiac, sending Jesse into a frenzy. He managed to free one of his hands from the stranger's chest. Jesse gripped the back of the biker's thigh, allowing him to hump that much harder, crushing his cock into the thick, muscled leg of his abductor.

The biker pulled his lips away. "Is that what you want? You want to cum now? We haven't even started. I'm going to bring you to heights of pleasure you can't even imagine. But if you cum in your pants now, humping my leg... it ends. Do you want it to end?"

Jesse heard the words, but they meant nothing to him. He'd become a cum hungry fuck animal. His hips flew back and forth, rubbing friction heat into his dripping cock.

"You whore." The vampire licked his lips. "Enough!" He jerked Jesse away from his leg, holding him at arm's length.

"Nooo..." Jesse whimpered. He'd been so close to cumming.

The hand grasping Jesse's hair forced him toward the filthy, grease-stained cement.

When the stranger unbuttoned the skintight jeans, instead of fighting, Jesse helped. And when the stranger's enormous erection sprang free, Jesse licked his lips.

"Suck," the biker commanded.

The cold, gritty cement of the abandoned warehouse hurt Jesse's knees. But the thick, circumcised magic wand inches from his lips had Jesse under its spell. The soft flesh of his lips touched the huge bell-shaped head. The biker's cock felt unexpectedly cool in the night's stifling heat. Jesse drew it into his mouth, savoring its salty essence. He wished he could unhinge his jaw like a snake, to take in the massive shaft.

The biker never let go of Jesse's hair. Instead, he pulled, forcing Jesse's struggling mouth further down the iron length of his perfect member. "That's it," he grunted. "You're doing such a good job."

Jesse's cock twitched in his shorts. The stranger's words felt so good. Tom never complimented him. Only berated him when he couldn't get Tom hard, or couldn't make Tom cum. In that moment, all he wanted was this stranger's praise... and his cock... and the ultimate compliment, his thick, salty cum.

And then the biker was pulling Jesse by his hair as he stepped back.

Jesse struggled to follow, mouth around the massive dick, knee walking with the dark muscled man.

The scent of hot metal accompanied the ticking of the cooling motorcycle as the stranger rested his ass on the edge of the seat, bringing his cock a little lower.

Jesse screamed around the thick cock in his mouth as his leg made accidental contact with the scorching exhaust pipe. As he did, the cock pushed deeper into him. The velvety skin of the stranger's balls touched Jesse's lower lip.

"Oh, fuck yes," the biker grunted. "Is that what it takes for you to open your throat for me?"

Jesse's leg was fiery agony. He placed his hands on the stranger's denim-clad legs and tried to push away.

"Suck me, you fucking whore!" the biker grunted, pressing Jesse's face into his salty skin, trapping his thick, hard meat deep in Jesse's throat.

Jesse thrashed. The corners of his vision blackened. And in those corners, Jesse saw others approaching. Men dressed just as this biker was. He struggled now in earnest, thrashing on the man's big dick.

The biker yanked Jesse's head back, pulling his dick from Jesse's mouth. A rough yank on Jesse's hair tilted his head up to meet those white eyes. "Good whore. But you haven't earned my cum yet."

The biker let go of Jesse then, pushed him back.

The others made no sound as they approached. Not the whisper of a breath, nor the tinniest scrape of their heavy boots on the gritty, stained cement.

Jesse turned in a circle, taking them in. Each and every man coming up on him was perfect. All of them just as handsome as the stranger that brought him here. They were all colors, from deep perfect obsidian, African skin, to the almost alabaster hues of arctic ancestry. They were maybe twenty in all. And every single one had those glowing white irises that seemed to command him. They dared Jesse to run. Some smiled, others licked their lips, and each showed the same sharp, ivory fangs as his nameless lover.

"Now is your chance, pet," his biker said. "Run along. Go back to your small, angry little boyfriend. Lie in the darkness tonight, nursing a black eye, crying into your pillow."

Jesse didn't move.

"Or stay," his handsome stranger continued, "worship perfection, and reap the rewards."

The others continued to get closer, forming a semicircle around Jesse, the biker, and the motorcycle.

Cold fingers of fear squeezed Jesse's heart. They were all so handsome, and so dangerous. Their eyes betrayed no kindness, only a burning passion behind their white-hot irises. "If I stay —" Jesse swallowed. "—will I survive?"

His biker reached out, grasped Jesse's chin in an iron grip, and pulled him close. "You won't survive, you'll *live*. Maybe for the first time in a long time. Isn't that better than surviving?" He smiled then, showing his fangs.

Entranced by the vampire's beauty, his confidence, his cock, Jesse nodded.

And then, he was being kissed again. The stranger's tongue parting his hot lips with its cool softness.

Hands grasped his shorts and underwear, pulling them down his legs. He tried to see who was undressing him, but the biker grasped Jesse's hair again, keeping him locked into the kiss.

Hands on his arms. More on his sides.

They ripped him away from his lover. Strong muscled bodies surrounded him, all dressed as his savior was, in leather vests open at the front, revealing six pack after six pack. They tore his shirt away. The press of their skin on his as they lifted him sent tingles of arousal through Jesse.

A dark-skinned man grabbed Jesse's cock and gave it a squeeze. More hands kneaded his ass. Fingers probed at his hole.

They laid him down atop the motorcycle. Jesse's shoulders rested on a pouch between the handlebars, his feet on the passenger foot pegs. His head fell backward.

A cock pressed against Jesse's lips. He opened his mouth, and was rewarded with a hard salty treat. The stiff shaft thrust forward, bumping Jesse's upside-down head against glass. Now he knew why they called it a *head* light.

Hands groped him all over. Stroking his cock, squeezing his balls. And cocks too, came in contact with his skin, rubbing and sliding against his stomach, his legs.

Cocks pushed into his hands, and Jesse stroked them, loved them, caressed them.

He sucked the cock in his mouth as best he could, upside down with no hands.

"Not good enough," an unfamiliar voice grunted.

"Hey!" an indignant cry came from somewhere near his head.

The dick slid from his mouth.

"Enough," it was the biker's voice. *His* biker's voice. "I brought him. I'm first. Give me some lube!"

Rough hands lifted Jesse's ass from the bike seat and smeared something slick between his cheeks.

Jesse raised his head to see his handsome biker. He sat astride the bike then and lifted Jesse into the air as if he were no heavier than a toy. Jesse reached out and caught his lover's shoulders. The hands on his ass guided him down until the tip of his savior's cock rested against Jesse's opening.

"Are you going to be good?"

Jesse nodded.

"Are you going to take all that I have to give you?"

Again, Jesse nodded.

"Say, yes Sir," the biker commanded.

Jesse wiggled his bottom, trying to get the cock without complying.

A sharp sting of pain exploded across Jesse's cheek. He hadn't seen the slap coming at all.

"Say it."

"Yes, S-sir," Jesse stammered. Heat bloomed, setting his face on fire.

"That's a good pet," the biker grunted, easing Jesse onto his pulsing staff.

"Ohhh," Jesse moaned. The big biker dick spread him and pushed him open. The delicious sensation of that masculine flesh filling him sent spasms to Jesse's neglected dick. It twitched in its sandwich of soft hair. The biker's on one side, Jesse's happy trail on the other.

"Yessss," the biker hissed, "Take it."

A hand took Jesse's and pressed a cock into it.

Jesse's biker nodded. "Stroke them. You must please them all before the sun comes up."

"Oooh..." Jesse's cock-dumb brain melted at the thought of pleasing so many men. Would they all use his ass? Or would he be able to use his hands and mouth to satisfy them?

As if his handsome stranger could read his mind, the biker said, "Tonight, your ass is only for me."

Handsome's statement left more questions than it answered. Jesse had no time to ponder such thoughts. Another cock pressed into his other hand.

Someone gripped his shoulders, pulling him backward. Again, his head came to rest between the handlebars. Insistent fingers gripped his chin, pulling his head back until once again Jesse was upside down. A girthy uncircumcised cock pressed against his lips, demanding entry. Jesse ran his tongue inside the velvety foreskin, reveling in the earthy taste, before allowing the salty, delicious rod between his lips.

"Yes," his biker cooed. "Look at you, you filthy fuck puppet, taking four cocks like a good boy." He pushed his big dick deep inside Jesse, all the while holding Jesse's hips, and pulling him down to meet each powerful thrust. "Fuck," the biker moaned. "Take it."

The handsome stranger's powerful cock bumped the special spot inside Jesse that sent tingles coursing up his spine. His fingers grew slick with the pre-cum from the cocks he jerked in each hand.

The guy fucking his mouth grew frantic. His thrusts came hard and fast, making Jesse choke on the cock lodged in his throat. The guy's big hairy balls slapped Jesse's face, blinding him. He grabbed Jesse's ears and grunted, "Suck me dry, you fucking slut!"

And just as Jesse thought he'd get a tasty reward, the guy pulled out. "I'm gonna fucking paint you!" he grunted, and started spraying Jesse's face, neck, and chest with a huge thick load of hot cum.

Before Jesse could see the man's face, another dick replaced the one in his mouth.

A hand gripped his, on either side, forcing him to speed up his strokes on the two cocks beside him. They came together. Sizzling hot drops of man-rain sprayed Jesse's stomach from both sides. As the bikers grunted their releases. Their moans of ecstasy echoed around the cavernous warehouse.

The guy who'd brought him to this sausage fest slowed his strokes inside Jesse's ass. "Good boy," he said, in a deep, strong voice. "Make them cum. Make them *all* cum!"

Fresh hard cocks replaced the spent dicks in Jesse's hands. And as they got into a rhythm, the rod in Jesse's mouth started pulsing. He sucked harder and tasted a single drop before the cocksman slapped his face. "Let go, you greedy fucking cum dumpster." He pulled his cock out and blasted Jesse's body with copious streams of sticky spunk.

The cum tickled as it joined the other loads on his skin and rolled, dripping from Jesse's exposed flesh. His cock pulsed and throbbed, bobbing up and down on his belly, neglected and aching. Before he could beg for someone to touch him, stroke him, and relieve the unbearable pressure building up inside him, yet another cock filled his mouth. The soft, salty foreskin wrapped around its hard, handsome head pulled back, allowing Jesse's tongue to caress its softness.

The biker fucking him built his speed again, causi ng Jesse's dick to bounce against his belly. Instead of providing the stimu-lation he needed, the sensation only teased Jesse to greater heights of arousal.

As before, hands tightly gripped his, directing his strokes on the pulsing cocks in his grasp, which did not help his state at all. The one on the left squeezed his hand and jets of cum splashed onto Jesse's aching dick. The hot spatter coated him from tip to balls, sliding down the side of his meat and pooling on his belly. Apparently, that was all the other guy needed. He bucked and shot his load all over Jesse's cock as well, covering Jesse's aching shaft in thick love juice.

Load after load splayed across his body, coating his crotch and torso. Cock after cock fucked his face until Jesse was sure he'd have black eyes from all the ball slapping. And each time, the guys pulled out and sprayed their nut all over Jesse's body.

He lost count of how many loads coated his skin and dripped onto the filthy cement. It wasn't until his hands and mouth were empty that the biker whose cock had remained hard and thrusting through it all, finally sped up his strokes again.

"Look at you, you filthy slut," he grunted. "You took nineteen fucking loads like the greedy whore you are. You look like a fucking glazed donut. You loved it, didn't you?"

"Ugh," was all Jesse could manage from his sore lips.

"Say it, slut. Say, I loved taking all that stranger cum."

Jesse, who remained upside down over the front of the bike, swallowed, and said, "I loved taking all that stranger cum."

"Good pet," the biker grunted. "You're going to walk home covered in all this cum. You're going to stagger down the street with twenty loads of fucking jizz mixed with dirt from the floor like the filthy whore you are. Understand?" the biker asked, clearly excited by the idea. His hands slipped a little as he shook Jesse's hips back and forth on his pulsing shaft. "Understand, bitch?"

"Y-es," Jesse moaned.

"Good boy. You're not going to touch your aching meat all day. You're going to walk all the way home covered in cum and dirt, with my load leaking out of your ass and dripping down your leg. You filthy fucking fuck slut!" The biker slammed Jesse against him, lifting Jesse's ass off the seat so that his gigantic balls spanked Jesse as they emptied all their pent up cum deep inside Jesse's hole.

Jesse moaned and whined in frustration as his cock bounced uselessly against his belly, aching for the stranger's touch. His tight ring gripped the biker's dick, throbbing in rhythm as the strong stranger filled his greedy hole.

Beams of moonlight sent diagonal silver shafts through a broken pane of glass. The light fell on Jesse's cum covered body. He tried to raise his head and found himself too tired to move. The only sounds in the room were his breathing and the slow drips of spunk splattering on the cement.

"I...." But Jesse was too cock-dumb to properly gather his thoughts.

"Hush," the biker said, lifting Jesse from his cock with impossible strength. "You did a good job. The others enjoyed playing with you. I'm proud of you. Rest now. I'll see you tomorrow after sundown."

Jesse tried to protest. To ask why he should. To ask the biker's name. But a mental fog descended. All he could manage to do was give a small nod.

He had the vague awareness of being laid out on the concrete.

CHAPTER

THREE

eat woke Jesse. A burning on his cock. His eyes refused to open at first. It took a moment to realize the reason, dried spunk from last night's festivities. When he managed to pry his lids open to half-mast, he found himself naked on the filthy cement floor of the abandoned warehouse.

"Oh, man," he said, staring down at the smeared dirt and peeling white flakes of dried cum covering his body. After sitting up slowly, Jesse surveyed the building. No sign of anyone else around. Trash on the floor. Some rusty machines in one corner of the warehouse, and rusty overturned lockers at the other end.

The heat on his cock came from the sun shining in through one of the broken windows high above. The rest were painted black. At least no one at street level could see in.

There was no evidence of his biker-man, the motorcycle, or the others. Just an empty warehouse. As he got to his feet, the cum the biker's cock left inside him dribbled out of his abused hole.

It felt weird, being naked and covered in dried cum in this

huge and unfamiliar space. Jesse didn't think he'd ever felt so vulnerable. The sensation of exposure, and the memories of being used by twenty gorgeous men sent a thrill through Jesse he would never have expected. And there was something else, something important about last night, hovering around the edges of Jesse's memory. It wouldn't come forward into the light of his conscious mind.

A quick search of the place yielded the clothes he'd worn to the club. They lay in a dirty heap, blackened from their contact with the floor, and covered in biker footprints. He slid them on, disgusted by the way the grit grated across his dirty skin.

The sensation of the cum flaking off of him reminded Jesse of the times in grade school when he'd covered his fingers in glue, then peeled it off. As he strode to the door, the biker's load seeped from his fucked-loose ass and trickled down his thigh. The sensation made his cock twitch in his booty shorts. He felt like such a dirty whore—and the feeling turned him on!

The weight of the phone in his shorts reminded him to check. He pulled it out. The battery sat at nine percent. Thirty notifications, all missed calls, texts, and messages from Tom. Shit. Tom was going to beat the fuck out of him. Literally.

He opened the door and stepped into the hot Vegas morning. When the rusty metal banged shut behind him, a young guy with pink spiky hair dressed in booty shorts, a fuzzy white vest that contrasted with his dark skin, and a pink scarf that matched his hair detached himself from the corrugated tin wall and approached.

"Hey," he said in a British accent.

"Uh, hey," Jesse replied, extremely conscious of how filthy and disgusting he must look. He took out his phone to call an Uber.

"Where are you going?" the guy asked.

"Um, what?" Jesse asked.

The guy huffed. "Where," he deflated and pinched his nose, "are you going?"

"H-home?" Why the fuck was this guy acting like Jesse had done something wrong?

"Did you just call an Uber, mate?"

"What, how?" Jesse stared at the guy.

"Did *he* tell you to do that?"

"I don't understand," Jesse said. He didn't. It was as if he'd entered some kind of bizarro alternate universe where men, sex, and mornings after made no sense at all.

The guy, who seemed barely old enough to have hair on his balls, spoke in slow halting phrases, as if he were speaking to a child. "Did the guy who brought you here tell you to call an Uber this morning?"

"I—"

The fuzzy vest didn't give him a chance to finish. "Or, did he tell you to walk home like this, with cum flaking off you and leaking out of your ass?"

"What the fuck—"

"Just answer the question, fuckmeat, okay?"

"I don't know who the fuck—"

"That's the first fucking right thing you've said." The guy stared at him with dark, intense eyes. "You don't know who the fuck I am, or who the twenty guys were that fucked you last night."

"I—" Jesse started.

"You don't."

This wasn't fair at all. "Who the fuck are you?"

"Ah," the guy held up a finger. "I'm the guy who's going to make sure you follow your fucking instructions."

"Look, I'm not going around...." Jesse started.

"Walk and talk, mate. It's hot, and I don't want to be walking around out here any longer than I 'ave to."

Jesse actually stamped his foot. "Not until you tell me who you are."

The guy raised an eyebrow. "Oh, so Ken's got some backbone."

"My *name* is Jesse."

"I called you Ken because you look like the doll. I know what your fucking name is."

"You do?"

"WALK, MOTHERFUCKER!" The guy screamed.

Jesse was so surprised by the sudden outburst that he started putting one foot in front of the other. He looked around for help, but the Arts District wasn't awake yet. The streets were empty except for the two of them.

"Better," Fuzzy Vest said, falling in step beside him. "Now. I'm going to walk ahead and take a little video for him, so he knows I did my job." The guy ran ahead, then walked backward, holding his phone up at Jesse. "That's so cool! The cum is making a clean track in the dirt on your leg as it drips down. He's going to love this!"

"He who?" Jesse asked.

"The guy that fucked all that cum into your filthy whore ass," the guy answered.

"Does he have a name?"

"Yeah," the guy replied, slipping the phone into his vest and falling in step beside Jesse again.

"Are you going to tell me what it is?"

"No," the guy said.

"I'm seriously thinking about calling the cops," Jesse said. His phone rang. Tom's ringtone.

"Don't answer that," the guy said.

"I'll fucking—" but Jesse didn't have a chance to finish.

Fuzzy Vest grabbed him by the throat, picked him off the ground one handed, and slammed his back against the wall of a shuttered bar. "You'll do what I fucking say. I'm the agent of the man who fucked you. For now, you can refer to him as Sir. I am his will, his instrument. His voice. And when he fucking painted your insides white last night, you became his. And so, you became mine, because I am also his. Get me?"

Jesse didn't. But he couldn't breathe. So he nodded.

Fuzzy Vest put him down.

Jesse put his hands on his knees, coughing and wheezing.

"Come on, candy ass," Fuzzy Vest said. He shoved Jesse forward.

"What's going on?"

The guy sighed. "You're walking home, like the filthy fuck-slut you are, covered in dried cum, with a load leaking out of your gaping ass, under my supervision. Fuck. I'm starting to think Sir was wrong, picking you. You might be too stupid for this."

"Picked me...." Jesse's mind swam. "Wait, too stupid for what?"

"Okay. Jesus. Look, you're Jessup Erich Fromm, social security number 000-112-2767, of 76 Mining Camp Ln. Sir picked you because you have only chosen family, and your partner is an abusive piece of shit. You've got a good IQ and a dead-end job." He poked Jesse's arm. "Right so far?"

He was. Right about everything. Jesse nodded dumbly.

"Right. And, you're pretty, like me."

Jesse held in a scoff. He was *way* better looking than Fuzzy Vest. The sun splashed down on them, cooking Jesse like a walking steak in booty shorts. His tongue was a dried-up prune in the desert of his mouth.

"I need water," he said. Also, he'd been sloshed when he fought with Tom, so that wasn't helping.

"Fair enough," Fuzzy Vest said. "I'm hungry. There's a diner up here."

"I can't go in looking like this," Jesse said.

As if to punctuate his point, a guy weaving down the street with a bottle and an army blanket over his head stopped to greet them.

"You'll go where I fucking tell you to go," Fuzzy Vest said. "Keep moving."

Honestly, Jesse wasn't sure if Fuzzy Vest meant him or the guy with the blanket. But his voice carried such authority, they *both* kept moving.

Inside, the waitress looked at them doubtfully.

By way of rebuttal, Jesse held up a wad of cash.

She shrugged, nodded, and led them to a table.

When they were seated, Jesse said. "Will you please explain what's going on?"

"Ok. Look, this is a trial run. Do what you're told today, and you'll never have to worry again."

"Can I get you started with something to drink?"

A gorgeous server stood at their table. His thin smooth arms clutched a pen and pad. But the twinky waiter wasn't looking at Jesse. Instead, the boy's eyes practically wept pre-cum as they drank in Fuzzy Vest.

"Hi," Fuzzy Vest said. "You could absolutely give me something to... drink."

The server cocked a hip, just so. Letting Jesse know he was playing the game. "What would you like? I've got a vanilla protein shake."

"I might like to 'ave a bit of that later. Just water for now, thanks."

The waiter nodded. "It's a desert out there. Got to stay wet on the inside."

Fuzzy Vest gave the waiter a dazzling smile. "I bet you are, love. I bet *you* are."

"Oh!" The waiter touched his fingers to his chest, returning

Fuzzy Vest's smile. He tucked the pad in his apron, frowned at Jesse, and departed.

"If I was going to kill you," Fuzzy Vest continued, as if the server had never been there at all, "why would I take you to breakfast?" Fuzzy Vest shook his head. "I thought you were supposed to be smart. No. I'm not going to kill you. You're going to serve Sir. You'll never have to worry about money, or a roof over your head. Never have to worry about your dickhead boyfriend smacking you around. Never have to worry about anything but doing what Sir says. Total freedom."

"Freedom?" Jesse asked. "That sounds like the opposite of freedom."

Fuzzy Vest shook his head. "It's the freedom from indecision, anxiety, worry, rent, bills, taxes. Sir will tell you what to do, where to go, what to think, all of it. You only need to comply with his every command, and you will live in comfort and luxury. Pretty good trade."

"What kind of whim?" Jesse asked, but he thought he knew.

"Like letting twenty of his biker friends cum on you and roll you in the dirt," Fuzzy Vest smirked.

Jesse's cock twitched in his shorts. He cast his eyes down to the filthy, flaky mess on his arms.

"You liked it, didn't you?"

Jesse raised his eyes. "Are you going to fuck me too?"

"If Sir wishes it. But mostly what I do for Sir is finance stuff. Logistics. Real estate acquisitions, like that warehouse."

"He *owns* that?" Jesse asked. "It's been abandoned for as long as I can remember."

Fuzzy Vest nodded. "It just *looks* abandoned. Sir *likes* it that way. Calls it his playpen." He gave Jesse a wolfish smile as he raised an engineer's boot to the seat between Jesse's legs and pressed the hard sole into Jesse's soft cock. "It's where he takes boys like you to play. Take you for a spin. And you liked it, didn't you?" His boot relented and pressed again, and again, forming a rhythm. "You liked the attention from all those guys, huh? Felt good to feel their cocks in your mouth, your hands, your ass. You liked gagging and choking on all those hot dicks. Feeling their cum spray all over you. Didn't you?"

Jesse nodded. He pushed back against the boot, using the delicious pressure to stimulate his growing erection.

"You like this, too, huh? Getting foot fucked in a crowded restaurant?"

Jesse cast his eyes around the place. There was definitely something perverse in sitting covered in dirt and flaking cum getting a foot job while grandmas ate pancakes at the next table.

"Hey, fuckwad?" Fuzzy Vest snapped his fingers and pushed his foot hard into Jesse's stiffening dick. "Over here."

Jesse dutifully returned his eyes to the Fuzzy Vest's sneering face.

"You didn't answer my question."

Jesse frowned.

Fuzzy Vest rolled his eyes and jammed his foot into Jesse's crotch. "This. You like this?"

A hot lance of pain shot through Jesse's crushed dick. He nodded, hoping compliance would stop the pain.

"Say it bitch." The guy cupped a hand to his ear.

"I like it," Jesse whined. His cock really hurt now.

"Not good enough. You like what?"

"I like getting foot fucked in front of grandmas eating pancakes."

"Oh!" The waiter set two glasses of water in front of them. He looked at the foot in Jesse's crotch, then at Fuzzy Vest. "Are you ready to order?"

"I'm always ready to order. Ain't that so, fuckwit?"

Jesse's face burned. He must be scarlet with embarrassment. The foot on his cock pressed harder.

"Ain't it?"

"Yes, Sir," Jesse managed through the delicious pain in his groin.

"I ain't Sir, now am I?"

"I don't know your name," Jesse groaned. Part of him wished for death. The part that was embarrassed to be seen filthy and cum covered in a restaurant. Getting foot fucked in front of a handsome waiter. But another part of him, the secret slutty part was ready to shoot the biggest load of cum into his filthy shorts, for the exact. Same. Reasons.

"That's right, love," Fuzzy Vest said. "You'll just take this abuse from any old bloke off the street. You filthy fucking whore."

The room receded around Jesse. He closed his eyes. His cock throbbed against the pressure of the lugged boot sole through the thin fabric of his shorts.

"Can I know your name?" the waiter asked.

"Of course, love."

Jesse opened his eyes to see the two men shake hands.

"It's Onyx," Fuzzy Vest said.

"Damien," the waiter said.

"Pleased to make your acquaintance, Damien," Onyx said. He threw an arm across the back of the vinyl seat as he continued to press and release his foot on Jesse's dick. "Did you know Damien comes from the Greek?"

"No, I—"

Onyx didn't give him a chance to finish. "It means to tame or subdue."

"I didn't know that," Damien said.

"Do you think you could tame or subdue this one?" Onyx inclined his head toward Jesse.

"Looks like he's already subdued," Damien said.

Onyx chuckled. "That he is. That he *is*." He punctuated his last 'is' by grinding his boot extra hard into Jesse's cock.

"Ugh," Jesse moaned. He didn't want to. He couldn't help it. It hurt so good.

"I need to see to the other customers," Damien said.

"Shame, that," Onyx said. "We'll each 'ave the protein breakfast. Sausage links, not patties and scramble the eggs, love. Oh, and I'll 'ave black tea. Black coffee for fuckwit here."

"I like cream and sugar," Jesse managed.

"No one asked you a fuckin' thing. You'll drink your coffee black and bitter this morning. And if you don't shut up, I'll stuff something else black and bitter in your mouth, and you'll get no fucking coffee. Am I clear?"

"Yes, sir," Jesse said. Then, hurriedly corrected, "I mean, Mister Onyx."

The foot on Jesse's junk eased up and went back to rubbing. The toes pressed and released the accelerator of Jesse's cock head inside his shorts.

"Good boy!" Onyx smiled for the first time since Jesse had met him. "Yes, very good boy. Maybe I can understand what Sir sees in you after all."

"I'll bring your food right out," Damien said. He gave Onyx a sly smile and departed.

Jesse's phone rang in his pocket again. Tom's ringtone.

"Is that your piece of shit boyfriend again?" Onyx asked.

Jesse nodded.

"Give it 'ere." Fuzzy Vest held out a hand.

As if in a trance, Jesse handed the phone over.

Fuzzy Vest tapped the screen, then held the phone to his ear. "Look, you useless waste of flesh. Consider yourself broken up wif. Jesse will be around to collect his things di-rectly. See that you stay the fuck out of 'is way."

Jesse grabbed for the phone, but Fuzzy Vest batted his hand away and crushed his cock with his boot.

"Who am *I*? You can call me Mister Onyx if you're fucking lucky." He paused, listening. "Well, if you're *unlucky* you can call me Mister, extremely violent and psychotic, who's going to put you in the fucking hospital. If I was you mate, I'd choose lucky." He lowered the phone and tapped the screen again.

"What the fuck," Jesse said. "Pick up my things? Where am I going?"

"Well, after we get your stuff from fuckstick's house, you'll stay with me until Sir decides what your situation will be."

"My situation?"

Fuzzy Vest, AKA Mr. Onyx, stared at him. "You know? Where you'll live, what you'll do for Sir, all that."

"I won't be living with Sir?" The whole conversation was ridiculous. Jesse knew it was. He went along with it as if it were totally normal to wonder where he'd be living from now on. What he'd do for work. His brain seemed to shut down on some level, wanting to accept this new turn of events. Wanting the so-called freedom Sir and Onyx offered.

Mr. Onyx shook his head. "*I* don't live with Sir. No one lives with Sir. He's an enigma. A ghost. I don't know where he lives, or what he does with his days. And no one I know does either."

Onyx pulled out his phone and ignored Jesse, all except his foot, which pressed and released Jesse's dick, keeping him on the edge of orgasm.

Jesse picked up his own phone.

"I didn't tell you to do that," Onyx said. "Turn it off and just sit there. Is my boot not good enough for you?"

Jesse held the power button, shutting his phone off. It only had three percent battery, anyway. "No, Mister Onyx."

Onyx looked up, surprised. "It isn't?" He jammed his sole into Jesse's crotch so hard it shoved Jesse back in the booth.

"I mean yes—"

"Fucking right it is," Onyx said, then returned his attention to the phone.

When their breakfast came, Onyx put the phone face down on the table. "Wanna see him do a trick?" he asked the waiter.

Damien cocked his head.

"Grab one of those sausage links in your filthy fingers and slide it into your mouth, nice and slow." Onyx pushed his foot harder into Jesse, letting him know the command was meant for him.

"They're too hot," Jesse protested, watching the steam rise from the meat.

"I don't fucking care. Let's see if you can, pet."

Jesse pinched the hot meat between his thumb and forefinger and raised it to his lips. It burned.

"Go on," Onyx encouraged.

Damien shifted his weight from one hip to the other and examined his nails. "How long will this take?"

"Now!" Onyx demanded.

Jesse licked his lips, hoping the spit would help cool the sausage. He slid the link forward. "Ow!" Reflex demanded he pull his lips back. The meat caught between his teeth.

"Now, now," Onyx said. "That's no way to handle a nice piece of meat. No teeth. You know that. Try again."

Jesse did. He gathered spit on his tongue and twisted the sausage as he slid it into his mouth.

"That's better," Onyx said.

"Nice," Damien said, "But he needs training, and I need to take care of the other customers."

"Stop back by," Onyx added, a playful lilt to his voice. "I think I can get him to take three sausages at the same time." He turned his attention back to Jesse. "Get that thing all the way into your mouth. I don't want to see that gray bit sticking out of your lips."

Jesse did his best, but the tip of the link kept hitting the back of his throat, triggering his gag reflex.

Onyx leaned in. "Now you listen 'ere. Sir isn't going to want to hear about how you couldn't hold one link of sausage in your mouth for a few minutes. After all, who wants a fuckboy who can't 'andle his meat, eh? Now you sit there just like that without gagging until I finish my eggs. If not, I'll drop you at Tom's to take the beating you so richly deserve, then go back to your shitty job. Or, you can suck that sausage like a cock for a few minutes and advance to the next level of existence." Onyx stuck a forkful of eggs in his mouth, then pointed the fork at Jesse.

The sausage tickled Jesse's throat. He slowed his breathing, trying not to think about it. Onyx's boot on Jesse's throbbing cock made the task all but impossible. This was all so wrong. The humiliation in front of the waiter should have wilted his dick. Instead, it made him diamond hard. Sitting here with a tube of breakfast meat in his mouth while Onyx ate, also turned him on. And Jesse was ashamed of himself, of his arousal by this bully, and that, too, got him off. The vicious cycle left his cock oozing pre-cum into his filthy shorts.

"That's a very good boy," Onyx declared when he'd swallowed the last of his eggs. "Now put another one in."

Jesse's mouth was too full to protest. He stared at Onyx.

"Go on, pet, do as you're told, or go home and get your beating."

Jesse picked up another link. At least it was cooler now. When he opened his mouth, he rushed his free hand to his lips to keep the first sausage from sliding out while he sucked in the second. Now that his mouth and throat were used to the intrusion, he didn't have any trouble with his gag reflex. The second link slid into his mouth without difficulty

"Why, you greedy little whore," Onyx smiled.

"How is everything here?" Damien asked as he sauntering up to the table.

"He's up to two," Onyx said.

Damien smiled. "Good for him. How's your meal?"

"Splendid." Onyx let his eye travel up and down Damien's body. "It's dessert I'm interested in."

Damien thrust his slender hips forward. "What can I get you?"

"How about a strip of Damien?" Onyx raised an eyebrow.

"Oh," Damien touched his fingers to his chest. "I've got a break coming up."

"I've got something coming up myself," Onyx said. Then he turned his attention to Jesse. "Hey fuckwit, put another sausage in."

ONYX MADE Jesse slide the sausages in and out of his mouth a few times while Damien watched. The cold greasy meat left a slippery, delicious coating on his plump lips. He never stopped jamming his foot into Jesse's leaking dick.

"Is he as good with the real thing?" Damien asked.

"Want to find out?" Onyx asked.

Jesse groaned around the slick meat in his mouth. He'd given up and given in. Twenty dicks last night, the promise of another right now, and no one had actually touched him. The closest thing he had was the rubber sole of Onyx's boot. His cock ached for real attention. Flesh. Lips. A soft, slippery asshole. Even just a leg to hump at this point. The idea of being used, of giving up all control, made him leak like a needy whore. And, he supposed he was.

Onyx allowed Jesse to scarf down his sausages and a few bites of eggs before standing and motioning Jesse out of the booth.

Jesse nearly wept when Onyx took his boot away. His cock throbbed and ached for attention.

"Don't you dare cover that wet bulge as we leave. I want all the grannies to see what a fuck-whore you are."

Fire rose in Jesse's cheeks as he stood. Black smeared boot prints emphasized Jesse's erection against the white fabric of his sparkly booty shorts. A wet spot the size of a silver dollar dotted the fat 'I' made by Onyx's boot print.

"Disgusting," a short-haired Karen muttered as Jesse passed her table.

"You should be ashamed of yourself," a silver daddy said. A bite of eggs dangled from his fork.

And, oh, Jesse was absolutely ashamed of himself. But the shame just made his dick harder. More needy. He imagined climbing under the table and sucking that guy off while the guy called him names and rubbed eggs in his hair. He imagined the salty taste of that self-righteous cock.

THE SUNLIGHT and the heat hit Jesse like a wall, sucking the moisture from his mouth.

Onyx led him around to the back of the diner. There, Damien stood smoking next to the cinderblock enclosure housing the dumpster.

"Ready?" Onyx asked Damien.

"Fuck yeah," Damien answered. He motioned to the dumpster. "Back here, away from the cameras." The stench of hot garbage hung thick in the desert heat as Damien led them behind the green, steel trash receptacle. Smashed, water bloated burger buns, sopping napkins, and unidentifiable filth marinated in a puddle of putrid trash-water.

Onyx pushed down on the top of Jesse's head. "Kneel."

"No, please," Jesse begged.

"Do it," Onyx commanded.

Jesse hated himself for wanting to obey, for wanting to be the most disgusting, depraved version of himself he could ever be. He loathed himself for his need. Something in him needed to know how far down he could go. How far he could let Onyx push him. All this and the promise of his handsome biker's approval brought Jesse to his knees in the wet, stinking garbage.

Damien freed his cock and brought it to Jesse's lips without ceremony. A stringy drop of pre-cum slid from where the tip peaked out of Damien's uncut foreskin.

Jesse extended his tongue, savoring the sharp taste and musky scent of Damien's dirty dick. He shoved the cock into his mouth, his tongue instantly sliding into the foreskin, seeking the strong musk of old sex.

Wet sounds above him made Jesse raise his eyes. Onyx and Damien leaned over him, their tongues intertwined. The sight of Onyx's dark lips locked onto Damien's pale pink flesh made Jesse's cock twitch in his pants. He didn't have time to enjoy more than a moment or two before Damien's hand grabbed a handful of Jesse's hair and shoved his cock down Jesse's throat until the trim patch of Damien's blond pubic hair tickled his nose.

The waiter's girthy shaft bumped the sore spot at the back of Jesse's throat, made tender by the dozen big dicks he'd swallowed the night before. The fat cock at the back of his throat brought a gag, a reflex Jesse had long thought he'd conquered.

"Oh, fuck yeah," Damien grunted. "It's so tight when you

gag." He pulled Jesse's hair harder, pistoning his head back and forth on his thick dick.

"I want to fuck you while he sucks you," Onyx said, yanking Damien's pants down. He grabbed Jesse's head, yanking it away from Damien's amazing cock. "Get him ready!"

Damien twisted, presenting his smooth, waxed ass to Jesse's eager tongue. "Lick out the load my boyfriend put there this morning!"

Jesse could taste it, the deep pungent scent of old cum mixed with the peppery essence of the twink's spicy hole. He pressed at Damien's tight ring then lapped along his crack, alternating between making his tongue hard and probing, or soft and wide.

Someone cuffed Jesse on the back of the head. "More spit, fuckmeat!"

The impact made Jesse's dick ache for attention. He felt so depraved, vile, and deliciously disgusting. So free. And as the taste of day old cum filled his head, he began to understand the freedom Onyx had talked about. Twenty loads of jizz cracked and flaked off skin, falling into the putrid dumpster water in a snowstorm of depravity.

Jesse reached a hand down to squeeze his needy dick.

"No one told you to touch yourself, fuckmeat," Onyx said.

Damien pulled away from Jesse's tongue and turned, presenting his throbbing shaft to Jesse's mouth again.

"Oh, fuck!" Damien grunted as he shoved his dick deeper into Jesse's mouth. "Not enough lube, you jerk!"

"Shut up and take it," Onyx grunted as he slid his shaft into Damien's ass.

Damien thrust his cock into Jesse's mouth with such violence, all Jesse could do was try to keep his mouth and throat open enough not to get hurt.

It didn't take long before both of the handsome men above him moaned.

"On his face!" Onyx said.

Damien's dick pulled away.

And while Jesse tried to catch his breath, hot drops of boy milk rained down on him from the two beautiful cocks pointed at his face. The cum spattered his cheeks, his hair, and his neck. Cum coated his lips, and a drop even landed in his ear. Jesse raised a hand to wipe away a drop on his brow that threatened to fall into his eye.

"NO!" Onyx commanded. You're going to do the walk of shame all the way to your ex-boyfriend's house.

New low unlocked. He'd have to face the world with two fresh loads of cum covering him.

"Clean us!" Onyx demanded, shoving his dark, thick shaft in Jesse's face. The remnants of his cum tasted sweet and spicy, reminding Jesse of leftover Thai takeout. He sucked eagerly on Onyx's softening cock, then licked up and down the shaft, greedily devouring any remaining trace of spunk.

"My turn," Damien said, playfully pushing Onyx away.

Onyx's cock came free of Jesse's mouth with a pop.

Jesse licked a drip of cum from his lips, then accepted Damien's softening dick between his mouth. Damien's jizz had a tangier, earthier flavor than Onyx's cum. Jesse sucked and licked the sticky, low-tide flavor from the velvety skin of Damien's shaft.

"I admit," Damien moaned, "he's got a mouth on him."

"That he does," Onyx said, slipping his cock back into his pants. "That he does. Okay, on your feet. Let's go. It stinks back here."

As Jesse stood, the trash water slid down his skin and dripped into his shoes. Neither of the other two men would look at him. Instead, they stood kissing while Jesse stood helpless in their spell. And while their tongues danced, Jesse's cock tented his shorts, and the filth dried on his skin. And when they were done sucking face, Onyx shoved Jesse forward, out of the dumpster's shade, and back into the blazing Vegas sun.

"See you around, sailor," Onyx called to Damien in his sexy British accent.

They walked on. Trash water squished in Jesse's shoes.

"Bloody hell." Onyx waved a hand in front of his nose. "You are proper pongy!"

"You're the one who made me——"

Onyx grabbed his hair, but kept their forward marching pace. "Just you remember your place. Wouldn't want to disappoint Sir, would you now? 'Course, you can bow out at any time. We're almost at your place. I could just drop you off, leave you with that abusive shit of an ex-boyfriend."

"I didn't say——" Jesse began.

"Then keep that tongue in your 'ead unless, of course, it's wrapped around a cock."

The sun dried the cum on his face. Jesse felt the skin tighten. Soon, it would start peeling and flaking from his face the way it was from the rest of his body.

Jesse's cock swayed gently back and forth as he walked, semi-hard and aching in his jockstrap. Pre-cum oozed from Jesse's dick, making a dark spot through his jock and filthy ruined shorts. His arousal at his sluttiness and situation kept blood flowing to his neglected cock.

FOUR

Outside Jesse's apartment complex, a big Hawaiian looking guy leaned against the wrought-iron fence. One massive sneaker rested on the bars, nearly bending them back.

"S'cuse me, gov'ner?" Onyx said, raising a hand toward the stranger like he was calling a server for another round.

The guy put his foot on the ground and straightened. "Me?"

"That's right," Onyx replied. "Fancy a bit o' work?"

"Do I look like I need work?" the guy scowled.

Onyx raised his hands. "No, sir, no, sir. But," he held up a finger, "you do look like a man who could use a blowjob."

"Name me a guy who doesn't look like he could use a blowjob?"

"Too right, too right," Onyx said. "But, the question stands, could you?"

"From who?"

"'im?" Onyx jerked a thumb at Jesse.

"He's disgusting," the big guy said.

"He's a filthy fucking whore," Onyx said. "Most of what you see isn't skin, it's cum."

"Even more disgusting. And you still haven't told me what the work is?"

"I'm stealing this one away, and I don't think 'is boyfriend will be too keen. Has a bit of a temper. Expresses emotion with his fists."

"What's it to do with me?" The big guy looked up and down the street. The sun blazed down on them.

Sweat dripped down Jesse's temple. It ran down his back and tickled the hair on the crack of his ass, mixing with the cum that still slipped around his hole, making him feel squidgy. The thought brought a fresh bit of blood to Jesse's dick. As did the thought of blowing the handsome island guy. Jesse loved big guys. He liked to feel small in the dominant presence of his lover. Feeling disgusting, depraved, and inferior added fuel to his forbidden fire.

"Well, I was hopin' you'd agree to come up and just keep things civil whilst we gathered this fuck-slut's things."

"And in return, he'd blow me? Is that the idea?"

"Somethin' like that, yeah."

"No way he could take me," the guy said.

"Care to place a wager?" Onyx raised an eyebrow.

"Alright," the guy said. "But if he can't make me cum down his throat, I get to cum in his ass. I'll literally tear him a bigger asshole."

"You're on," Onyx said.

"Hey!" Jesse protested.

"Shut up, fuckmeat. Let's go see your boyfriend."

The big guy's footsteps thundered in the enclosed staircase leading to the apartment Jesse shared with Tom.

Jesse, of course, had no keys. No wallet either. It was the way Tom insisted he live: totally dependent on Tom for everything from buying drinks and food, to rides, to just getting into his own fucking house. Jesse knocked.

Tom answered the door looking like absolute shit. His hair was a mess. Dark circles ringed his monkey-shit-brown eyes. "Where the *fuck* have you been?" He glanced at Onyx and the big dude. "Who the fuck are *they*?"

"We," Onyx answered before Jesse could gather his thoughts. "Are your two biggest fucking problems at the moment, gov'na." Onyx said.

Tom reached for Jesse's wrist, presumably to yank Jesse to Tom's side of any ensuing conflict.

The big dude wagged a kielbasa finger. "Don't."

"Do you know what this little fuck stick did?" Tom asked.

"Put up with your abuse way longer than he should 'ave," Onyx spat.

"What?" Tom's face wrinkled up like a baboon's ass. "He fucking took off and left me at the club and now he shows up, what? Eighteen hours later with you two assholes. My god," Tom wrinkled his nose.

"Step out of the way mate, we're coming in to gather 'is things." Onyx jerked a thumb at Jesse.

"The *fuck* you are. You—" Tom started, but the sound of the big guy slapping a ham hock sized fist into his open palm brought him up short.

Onyx put a hand on the small of Jesse's back and pushed him into the room.

Tom stood aside, dumbfounded expression on his face.

"Got a suitcase?" Onyx asked Jesse.

Jesse nodded. He couldn't make his lips work.

"Get it," Onyx said. "Just your favorite clothes and things."

His stomach roiled, and his gut clenched. It felt as if his intestines were knotting themselves up. What if Tom came after him? What if Onyx let that happen? What if the big guy started beating the shit out of Tom? In spite of everything, Jesse loved Tom, didn't he? After all, Tom was his shelter. His rock. Tom provided for him and protected him from everything in the big bad world... well, everything but Tom. And if he got angry and lost control sometimes, that was okay, wasn't it? After all, Tom didn't mean it. He always made up and brought Jesse flowers or a nice dinner after. Having to wear sunglasses in public once in a while was a small price to pay.

Except, no. It wasn't. Deep down, Jesse knew that. He knew Tom was a toxic abuser. And somehow, he couldn't bring himself to leave. What was the point? Tom would find him, and then... oh man. That scenario was bad news.

"What the fuck is all over you—" Tom started.

"It's cum," Onyx said. "A fucking lot of cum."

Tom's mouth dropped open. And when Jesse walked past, Tom gagged. "Oh fuck, did you spend the night in a dumpster?"

"He blew my mate behind one," Onyx said, following Jesse to the bedroom.

"Hey, you're not actually doing what this prick says!" Tom shouted as Jesse pulled his suitcase from the closet.

Part of Jesse's mind couldn't believe he was following Onyx's commands, either. He plopped his suitcase on the bed. Hazy yellow sunlight lit the dust motes that danced in a snow flurry from the disused luggage. Another part of his mind, though, knew it was time. Time to get out of this toxic relationship. And into another? What the fuck? He'd allowed himself to be used by twenty guys last night, plus two more today. He hadn't asked anyone if they had been tested for STIs. Hell, he hadn't asked anyone's name. He only knew Onyx's name because he'd heard Damien ask. And he only knew Damien's the same way. But, no one had hit him. And, honestly, he'd been given a choice at every step. The handsome stranger had given him the choice to walk away last night. And Onyx gave him a choice this morning. Whatever this was, he'd done it all of his own free will, which was more than he could *ever* say about Tom.

"You know," Jesse said, withdrawing a pile of his favorite clothes from the hangers in the closet. "I am following this guy's instructions. I want to. And I don't want you, Tom. Not anymore."

"Now you wait—"

"No," Onyx cut Tom off. "You wait. Did you 'ear what he said? He don't want you anymore. Don't need you, see."

"Fuck. You." Tom said. He took a step toward Jesse, lips curled into a snarl.

The big man grabbed Tom.

Tom tried to shrug off the giant, but the big man dug his hands into Tom's shoulders, holding him in place.

"Get off me!" Tom shrieked.

"Don't test him, mate. You'll fail," Onyx said.

"Get. The. Fuck. Off. Me!" Tom grunted and pushed and struggled in the big guy's grip.

"This guy isn't going to stop," the big man said.

Jesse paused with a pile of clothes in his hand. He looked from Tom to the giant, to Onyx.

Tom's eyes flashed with the anger that had nearly sent Jesse to the hospital more than once. He only focused on Jesse for a moment. But that was enough. His eyes told the story of how he'd hurt Jesse if he ever got free.

Before Jesse was aware of it, he was behind Onyx, peeking over his shoulder.

Onyx pinched the bridge of his nose. "Bloody hell! We're never going to get out of here at this rate." He pointed at Tom. "You're going to shut the fuck up, or here's what's going to happen: We're going to call the cops, see. And we're going to say that you did this to 'im. See what happened is, we was walking by your apartment and we 'eard Jesse callin' for help.

We busted in, and found you hittin' him. Turns out you won't let him wash up, just like fuckin' 'im and beating 'im." He turned to the big guy. "Ain't it so?"

The big guy nodded. "That's what happened."

"Hang on—"

"I don't fink I will 'ang on. I fink you either shut up or go to jail. Now what's it going to be?"

Tom said nothing.

"Ahhh, peace and quiet," Onyx said. He turned to Jesse. "Go on then. Don't want to be 'anging around here all day."

Jesse put the clothes in the case. As he did, he cast his eyes to the big stranger. The big man stood looking at Jesse, rubbing the huge bulge in his board shorts.

"How does he suck?" the man asked.

"Like a champ," Onyx answered.

Jesse's cock stirred. The butterflies in his stomach told him he was suddenly free. His eyes fell on Tom's.

His ex-boyfriend's soul windows brimmed with anger and hurt.

Although Jesse was following the commands of Onyx, that was his choice. Doing what Tom said had always been out of necessity. This was, different. Free somehow.

"You remember our deal?" The big guy asked.

"Of course," Onyx replied. "He'll suck you good, I promise."

"He'd better!" The giant replied, "or I'll ruin his hole." He unbuckled the leather belt straining to contain his thick hips.

Jesse licked his lips as the black fabric of the man's shorts parted to reveal the fattest cock Jesse had ever seen, and he'd seen quite a few. The dark, angry head of the stranger's dick was as wide around as a soda can.

"Time to earn your protection," Soda Can grunted.

"Go on," Onyx prompted. "We'll come round and get the rest of your things later."

"What about Tom?" Jesse asked. He wasn't sure he'd survive an encounter with Tom alone.

"Oh, I've got special plans for our old friend Tom, just you wait and see. In between whiles, go on and take care of our big friend over there. Show 'im your talents."

Tom opened his mouth, but snapped it shut when Onyx held out his cell phone.

Jesse did as instructed, walking over to Soda Can and kneeling in front of him.

"No," Soda Can instructed. "Over Tom's face." He looked at Tom. "Lie down."

Anger flushed Tom's cheeks crimson. He didn't move.

"I could always knock you out and tell the cops I was coming to his aid," Soda Can said, jerking a thumb at Jesse. "It would make things easier, if a lot less fun."

Tom set his jaw, his face a mask of malice as he lay down on the floor.

Jesse knealt with his knees on either side of his ex-boyfriend's head, and Soda Can stood, with the tips of his sneakers touching Jesse's knees.

The big man's hard cock wagged in Jesse's face. The musky scent of Soda Can's shaft entered Jesse's nose and traveled to his groin, sending a fresh spurt of blood to his aching dick. Jesse extended his tongue, giving the fat cock a tentative lick. The salty tip tasted of earth and mushrooms.

"Go on," Soda Can urged. "Your mouth or your ass. Your choice."

No way he was fitting that thing in his mouth without lube. Jesse licked his lips, then gathered spit on his tongue and dragged it up and down the thick barrel of the Soda Can's cock. Thick as it might be, at least it wasn't super long, otherwise Jesse was sure he'd need surgery to get the massive dick dislodged from his throat. Jesse opened as wide as he could, curling his lips around his teeth.

The big guy grabbed the back of his head and slid his enormous slab of meat into Jesse's mouth. "Oh!" He grunted. "So fucking tight."

Jesse willed his gag reflex into submission. He was going to need this guy to cum quickly. His jaw ached, stretched to its maximum. Plus, the big guy was right, if he fucked Jesse, he might end up in the hospital. Jesse pushed up on the underside of the guy's shaft with his tongue, massaging the underside of the dude's head and frenulum with quick strokes, pushing the top of the intruding cock head into the ribbed roof of his mouth.

The big man grunted again and began thrusting his hips. His hands grasped handfuls of Jesse's blond hair, and he fucked Jesse's mouth. "Oh, that fucking tongue is magic. He should give classes."

"Right?" Onyx chuckled. "Now you see why he's coming with me. Too much talent to waste on that asshole."

Out of the corner of his eye, Jesse saw Onyx indicate Tom.

Jesse squeezed as best he could with the hot beer can sized tube of man meat in his mouth. His breath came in quick gasps through his nose.

The big man's cock oozed copious pre-cum, making Jesse's mouth that much slicker.

Jesse reveled in the delicious sweet-n-sour taste of the guy's leaking dick.

Soda Can grasped Jesse's hair even tighter as his hips pumped faster. His dark, sparsely haired belly bumped Jesse's forehead with every thrust of his fat, fat cock.

The muscle of Jesse's tongue strained to keep the pressure up. He batted side to side as the cock slid across it.

"He's never going to make me cum this way," the big guy groaned.

"Better up your game," Onyx admonished. His voice held a mischievous lilt.

Jesse redoubled his efforts. His tongue and jaw screamed in agony. The thought of this guy shoving his colossal dick in Jesse's tight boy hole scared the hell out of him. It also tickled a deeper place. A depraved place in Jesse's mind. Taking that monster dick in his ass would make Jesse the ultimate slut. The ultimate submissive. The biggest man-whore in Las Vegas. And, something inside him wanted the title, no matter what it cost him. No matter how it hurt. And, the thought of that pain, to Jesse's surprise, made his cock ache in his shorts. His head rubbed back and forth along the underside of his waistband, lubed by copious pre-cum. Jesse bucked his hips in the air over Tom's face.

Thinking of Tom under him, watching Jesse try to take that massive dick, a dick way bigger than Tom, heightened Jesse's excitement. Jesse eased up on his efforts to make the enormous dick in his mouth cum.

"Nah," the big guy said. "He's running out of steam. I think it's time to try his other hole."

"Well," Onyx said. "We never really set a time limit or anything."

Out of the corner of his eye, he saw Onyx rubbing the crotch of his shorts. "Sorry love, you lose this one, I'm afraid."

The big guy pulled Jesse's hair, yanking his head back. The guy's big cock slid from Jesse's mouth with a pop. "On your feet, but don't move from that spot."

Jesse wanted that massive dick, but knew he'd need a little help. "There's lube and poppers in the bedside table."

"Hmmmm," Onyx rubbed his chin. "You've been a good boy today—"

Jesse's cock twitched with the praise.

"I suppose that'd be alright." Onyx retrieved the bottles

from the drawer. "'ere." He handed the lube to the big guy and held the other bottle. "Suck my cock whilst he gets you ready. I'm sick of just watching the show."

Jesse bent over with the crotch of his filthy shorts right over Tom's face. This felt so wrong and depraved, yet, so, so fucking right. Tom liked to watch, but only when he was in control of the scene, in control of Jesse. Now all he could do was watch as two guys way more handsome with way bigger dicks used him.

"Don't move, Tom. Don't speak and don't touch yourself, or I'll kick your ugly fucking head in," the Soda Can growled.

"See that you follow 'is instructions, mate," Onyx admonished. "Or it'll go badly for ya."

The big guy yanked Jesse's shorts to his thighs, giving him access to Jesse's horny hole. To Jesse's disappointment, the big guy didn't pull them down far enough to free Jesse's needy cock. Instead, Jesse's cock oozed more pre-cum into his shorts. The need to cum had been building all day, and Jesse craved any pressure on his dick.

As if reading his mind, Onyx wagged a finger in Jesse's face. "Remember what Sir said. If you cum, it's over. I'll leave you wif 'im." Onyx waved the bottle of poppers in Tom's direction.

The warning was enough to cool Jesse, making his cock relax a notch, and not rub the fabric of his shorts.

As Onyx unscrewed the cap on the poppers, Soda Can smeared lube on Jesse's ass, roughly jabbing a finger into the entrance to Jesse's hole. The intrusion made Jesse draw a sharp breath. When that happened, Onyx stuck the bottle of poppers into Jesse's face. The vapor flooded Jesse's nose. His body tingled. His heart raced. And his ass relaxed just in time to feel the head of the big guy's massive member knocking on his back door.

Onyx freed his impressive cock and pressed it to Jesse's lips. Jesse's lovers pushed their dicks inside him at the same time. Even with the poppers and the excitement of showing off for his prone ex-boyfriend, the big guy's huge girth *hurt* going in. Jesse grunted in pain around the salty skin of Onyx's dark, delicious shaft.

"That's it," the big guy growled. "Take it like a good boy." He didn't move, giving Jesse's straining hole time to get used to the unbelievably big intrusion.

How could the big guy know how much Jesse loved being called a 'good boy'? How those words ran straight through him, relaxing his ass to meet the girthy cock inside him. The big guy's approval eased his pain and made Jesse refocus his efforts on Onyx's veiny, velvet shaft.

Onyx took the opportunity to grab Jesse's hair and guide his dick deeper into Jesse's throat. "That's right. Don't forget there's two of us 'ere, fuckmeat."

Jesse's head swam as much from the poppers and sudden lack of air as it did from the mix of pleasure and pain these two huge dicks caused him.

"Steady," Onyx said, grasping Jesse's curls tighter, and placing a steadying hand under Jesse's armpit.

The pain in Jesse's ass receded, replaced by the delicious feeling of being stuffed more than he ever had. He thanked the universe once again that the big guy behind him wasn't long, just thick. This allowed Jesse to push his whorish hips back with confidence, seeking the wonderful feeling of his lover's sparsely haired belly on the skin of his cheeks. He couldn't say why, but that skin on skin, belly to ass contact, made him feel safe and loved.

"Cup my balls, dickpuppet," Onyx admonished.

Jesse took a hand from his thigh and held Onyx's velvety sack.

"Don't cum inside him," Onyx said to the guy fucking Jesse. "That honor is reserved for his master."

"Where?" the big guy asked.

"Half on his ass," Onyx directed. "And half on 'is boyfriend's face."

The big guy chuckled. "You guys are fucked up. I'm here for it."

Jesse moved his hips to meet his big lover's increasing thrusts. And Onyx matched them both. They became a three dicked fuck machine. Jesse wished Tom could reach up and stroke Jesse's needy cock, instead of having it bob, neglected and useless, in the filthy fabric of his shorts.

The room filled with the musky smell of manly sweat. Jesse's ass made obscene squishing, squelching sounds as he struggled to take the ferocious pounding Coke Can dished out. Jesse's spit mixed with Onyx's salty pre-cum dribbled down his chin as Onyx forced his perfect cock down Jesse's throat.

As the two men worked his holes, he imagined the look on Tom's face. Imagined his lovers lifting him off the ground with their cocks, rotating him in the air like a fuck-pig on a spit, making him their cock sleeve, their meaty meal.

And through the squelching, gagging, drooling, sucking sounds, a familiar noise reached Jesse's ears. It was the chuffing grunts Tom made when he beat his meat. Jesse couldn't see his prone ex-lover on the floor, but could well imagine Tom stroking his cock to the sight of the Soda Can's balls slapping Jesse's as the guy's fat fucking shaft augered into his abused rectum.

It thrilled him to act like a total whore in front of Tom, knowing that Tom could never touch him again.

The guy behind Jesse grunted and pulled his cock out, leaving Jesse empty and gaping.

"I'm gonna fucking paint you white!" the guy grunted.

Hot cum sprayed all over Jesse's exposed ass. Onyx pulled

his cock from Jesse's slackened mouth and began spurting thick ropes of cum into Jesse's upturned face.

The big guy kept cuming and cuming, blasting Jesse's cheeks, crack, and gaping hole with hot jizz. It ran a river down his crack, his balls, and finally dripped onto his ex-lover.

Jesse slid his hand from Onyx's heavy balls, grasping the man's thick shaft and rubbing it on his face. He lifted his head higher, cradling the dark sensuous shaft in the crook where his neck met his jaw. He delighted in the feeling of a cock there. The last pumps of Onyx's cum slid down Jesse's neck, cooling as they ran down his chest under his loose, torn shirt, stiffening his nipple.

Fuck. This was sooo hot, and he needed to cum sooo fucking bad. Jesse's cock ached in his shorts. Flopping around in the fabric.

"Suck it clean," Onyx said, taking his dick from Jesse's desperate grasp and shoving it back in Jesse's mouth. "You eager fucking whore. Unbelievable."

"He's good," Soda Can agreed.

"Oh fuck!" Tom grunted.

"Hands off, or he'll kick your head in!" Onyx shouted. "Ruin your orgasm you piece of shit!"

Jesse looked down to see Tom's familiar cock bobbing in the air, spraying jet after jet of cum all over his black T-shirt. The urge to grasp and stroke that delicious meat was almost too much for Jesse to handle. He could just squat right down and take that dick into his loose hole. One or two strokes on his own dick and Jesse could release the fucking ocean of cum his swollen balls could barely contain at this point. But no. No orgasm was worth that. No amount of cum or quick satisfaction could ever make Jesse go back to that life.

. . .

"Fuck me that's just what I needed!" the guy said. "Clean me up, bitch."

"Do it," Onyx said, spinning Jesse around.

Below him, Tom lay, eyes wide with fear, face covered in the big guy's spunk. Jesse barely had time to wonder how the big man had managed to cover both his ass and Tom's face. The guy must have cum a gallon.

He hesitated as the Soda Can fed him that fat, wide dick. The peppery taste of his own ass made Jesse's tongue tingle. He'd never done ass to mouth before. New low unlocked. And the idea of that, made Jesse's lonely cock twitch.

Behind Jesse, Onyx tugged the waistband of Jesse's shorts, tucking his balls back in before yanking the soiled fabric back to Jesse's waist, trapping all the big man's cum in Jesse's crack and on his balls.

Jesse licked back and forth on the big guy's shaft, sucking up what he found there and swallowing it down.

"This guy's going to get me hard again already!" the big man said in disbelief.

"That's enough, fuckmeat," Onyx said. "Any more and you'll have to satisfy him again."

Jesse stopped in mid lick. No way was he in for that right now.

"Look at his pants." The guy nodded toward Jesse.

Jesse's eyes fell. His cock made a big tent in his shorts. A copious collection dark cum spots stood out among the other stains.

"He is a propper whore," Onyx agreed. "Loves 'is work."

"What about him?" the big guy asked, nodding at Tom. "He wasn't supposed to touch himself?"

"Too right," Onyx said. "Hmmm. Very naughty Tom. You'll 'ave to pay for that." He turned to Jesse. "Do you have a really big suitcase?"

Jesse nodded and pulled down the giant soft sided bag Tom bought when they were going on their two-week gay cruise the year before.

"Perfect," Onyx said. He turned to the big guy. "Think you can fit Tom in there without breaking any bones?"

The guy frowned and scratched his chin. "Maybe."

"Hey!" Tom yelled, getting to his feet.

"Night-night asshole," the big guy said, and clocked Tom in the jaw.

Tom fell forward, landing face-down, half on and half off the bed.

The big guy balled Tom up and stuffed him in the case, squashing the top to zip it. "Not bad."

"Good," Onyx said. "We'll take him with us."

The big guy nodded.

Minutes later, they were on the sidewalk by the guy's big black sedan. The big guy tossed the bag with Tom inside roughly into the trunk. "Maybe send him back up to get a sheet or something," the guy said. "I don't want him fucking up my upholstery."

"Do it," Onyx said. "And be quick about it."

Jesse ran back up, and rather than finding a fresh sheet in the closet, he ripped the top sheet of the bed. He'd always hated these floral sheets Tom insisted on using.

If Onyx had told the coke can cocked guy where they were going, he must have done it while Jesse was upstairs. Because once the sheet was spread across the back seat, Onyx got in the passenger seat, and the big man pulled out into traffic without a word.

Jesse knew better than to ask where they were going.

FIVE

I nside the warehouse, Jesse had little time to search for the tracks and drippings of the previous night's festivities in the gathering darkness. Onyx strode briskly with swishing his hips across the dusty cement floor, and Jesse hurried after. He led Jesse through a door at the back of the warehouse. There he stopped, turned and approached Jesse. "You did well today. I think Sir will be most pleased."

Jesse flinched and took a step back. His mouth hung open.

Onyx grasped his hand. "It's okay. Come."

The uncharacteristic praise, kind tone, and shocking touch of Onyx's smooth fingers on his made Jesse question his grasp on reality.

The brass skeleton key Onyx produced from his vest pocket glittered in the darkness. Onyx unlocked the door one-handed and tugged Jesse through. Only the dark-skinned man's bright clothes distinguished him from shadow in the darkness beyond. Jesse couldn't figure out how the beautiful man found his way in the inky obscurity at first. Gradually, as his eyes adjusted, a faint orange glowing line at the end of the hallway resolved out of the black. As they approached, Jesse realized it must be candle or firelight coming through a crack at the bottom of the door.

As Jesse's eyes adjusted further. Peeling, minty faded paint chips curled off the walls and littered the floor. The only sound in the passage was their shuffling feet, and Jesse's ragged, nervous respiration.

Without letting go, Onyx unlocked the door before them.

The light in the room almost hurt Jesse's eyes after the darkness. A hundred candles in candelabras lit the posh chamber. Where on the other side of the door, the squalor and decay belied a haunted asylum, on this side of the door, the splendor and opulence gave the impression of a five-star hotel before the advent of electricity. Arranged about the big room were Victorian sofas with thick velvet cushions. The scrollwork in their dark, lustrous wooden frames reflected the candles in glittering points of light.

Arranged on the sofas, the bikers from the night before sat in dark suits, some with tails and top hats. Near the center of the room, a single high back chair faced the entrance. In it lounged his biker, puffing on another clove cigarette. A cloud of shadowy smoke rose around him.

Onyx pulled him to face his handsome biker, now adorned in a tuxedo reminiscent of the 1930s with its ruffled shirt and thin lapels. When Onyx stopped, they stood on a thin mesh grate in the floor about three feet square.

His biker broke the silence. "How did he do?"

Onyx tried to let Jesse's hand go, but Jesse's fingers refused to relinquish the affirming contact.

"It's okay," Onyx assured him, grasping Jesse's wrist and squeezing until Jesse let go. He turned to Jesse's biker and knelt on the grate. "Sir. He did very well. His initial resistance was about what we've come to expect. Once we got beyond that, his obedience and enthusiasm were top of his class."

"How about his skills?" The biker asked.

"He has excellent oral skills, even under the most difficult circumstances," A familiar voice answered behind Jesse. "His sucking, deep throating, and tongue work are ten out of ten. Hell, he even got me off despite the stench that—" Damien stopped short, obeying Sir's tiniest gesture, a wagging finger. "Sorry."

It was Damien. Holy shit! What was *he* doing here?

Jesse resisted the temptation to turn, but he let his eyes travel over the erstwhile waiter, now dressed in a tuxedo sans shirt. Jesse's mouth watered at the memory of the handsome twink's delicious cock. He licked his lips.

Sir roused from his relaxed attitude, leaning forward, hands on his knees, staring at Jesse with those gorgeous white irises. "It seems our young thrall is hungry for it again." He raised a finger and pointed to the left side of the gathering circle of vampires. Even in the dimness, their bulges stood out of their dark suit pants. "Kai, report."

Jesse gaped as the big guy who'd been standing outside of Tom's apartment house stepped forward. "As you are prepared to hear, Sir, his tongue is excellent. And though he resisted at first, his obedience is top-notch. He took me in both holes without much protest. He cleaned my dirty cock with fervor and precision."

Jesse's cock bulged in his shorts. The memory of tasting his own ass on Soda Can's dick set Jesse's meat twitching. Butterflies fluttered through his stomach as the feeling of submission and depravity returned.

Jesse's cock dumb brain struggled to put all this in context. Soda Can/Kia, Damien, Onyx this... this whole thing had been planned. It wasn't spontaneous. He hadn't been made to service random strangers after all.

"I see the truth is starting to register, Jesse," the head

vampire fixed Jesse with those glowing white eyes and a mischievous smile that showed his fangs. "These men are free of disease. Safe." The vampire looked first to Kai, on Jesse's left. Then glanced at Damien on Jesse's right. "Did he even ask?"

"No, Sir," Kai responded.

"No, Sir," Damien echoed.

"Well, not surprising after he jumped on my motorcycle last night without knowing where I would take him. Who I was." The vampire turned his eyes back to Jesse. "That is the only area where you are found wanting. As my thrall, you are expected to remain faithful to me. Any dalliance with other men... could prove fatal. As could evidence of such a coupling in the form of an STI. Fatal. You understand?"

Jesse swallowed hard, then nodded.

"Speak!" the vampire commanded.

"Y-yes, Sir." Jesse's cock ached.

"Very well. Jesse, as my thrall, you will serve my interests in the world of men, in finance, business, and the care of my dwellings. You will receive a generous stipend. You will want for nothing. The price is absolute obedience." The head vampire rose from his high-backed velvet chair and stood in front of Jesse. "Absolute obedience," he repeated in a softer tone. "And besides the creature comforts I have mentioned, you will also receive my love and affection. Sometimes this will take the form of cuddles, kisses, and fucking. Sometimes my love... hurts. Do you understand?"

"Yes, Sir," Jesse said without hesitation. He wanted all of it. He wanted the love, and kisses, and cuddles, and fucking. He wanted the pain, humiliation, and... punishment. And most of all, he wanted to cum staring into those white, vast, sexy eyes.

"So it shall be," his handsome vampire said. He reached out a hand, then drew it back. "You stink of old cum and garbage. It won't do. Rise."

Jesse stood.

"Strip!" his sexy vampire commanded.

Jesse peeled off his shorts and shirt. His erection bobbed free. A long string of pre-cum drooled from his tip, reaching for the floor.

"Kai, Damien, prepare him," the vampire said, returning to his throne.

Beside him on the grate, Kia and Damien removed their clothes. A thrill of validation shook Jesse when he noticed their cocks were hardening, too.

Fresh warm water showered down over them.

Jesse held his new master's eyes as the soapy, slick hands of his erstwhile lovers traveled his body, washing the filth and dried cum from his skin. Standing naked, stripped bare of all dignity in front of this powerful creature and all these other strangers excited Jesse further. His cock bobbed and ached with the need he'd built up for the last twenty-four hours.

When a soapy hand traveled down the length of Jesse's needy shaft, his knees quaked. A moan escaped his lips.

"Don't you dare cum!" his master commanded.

"Close your eyes," Kai whispered.

Jesse obeyed.

Someone lathered his hair, while another set of hands spread his ass cheeks and probed his hole with slick fingers.

Jesse's hips thrust back in a silent plea for penetration.

"Tsk, tsk," Damien said. "This is a cleaning, not a fucking. You belong to Sir, now."

Jesse whined behind lips closed to keep the soap out.

Buckets of warm, luxuriant water rinsed his hair.

"Open your mouth," Kai commanded.

Jesse did, and a toothbrush covered in minty gel attacked his teeth. And something about this too, having his teeth brushed as he stood helpless before his master, excited Jesse, as if he couldn't perform the most basic functions on his own anymore. The absence of freedom and responsibility relaxed him and aroused him at the same time.

As if reading his thoughts, his master commanded, "open your eyes."

Jesse did.

The lord vampire, his Master, locked his gaze on Jesse as Kai aggressively scrubbed Jesse's mouth with the rough bristles.

"Spit," Kai commanded.

But Jesse made no move to comply until his new master gave a faint nod. Implied permission for Jesse to break eye contact, lean over, and expectorate the foamy white fluid down the dark grate at his feet.

When the two men who'd used him roughly all day had scrubbed Jesse from tip to toe, asshole to elbow, the water stopped, and Jesse stood shivering in the candlelight.

The vampire in the chair held his arms out. "Come."

As if in a trance, Jesse stepped off the grate and approached the chair.

Sir held a hand up over his shoulder. One of the tuxedo clad vampires behind him placed a large, fluffy, black towel in it. Sir spread the towel over his lap and patted his knee.

Jesse sat, not breaking eye contact. When his bottom and balls met the soft fabric, sir wrapped the rest of the towel over his shoulders.

"You've done so well," he said. "Rest your head on my shoulder."

Jesse did, drinking in the strong musky essence his new master exuded.

A vampire whose skin was so dark it gleamed purple in what little candle light it failed to absorb stepped forward. He held a book open in his palms. "Do you, Vitus, Lord of the Las Vegas coven, mightiest of the vampires, take Jesse as your thrall, to use and control as your servant, slave, and proxy in worldly affairs? Do you swear to fulfill all the needs of his body, mind, and spirit until his death, or such time as you grow tired of him?"

"I do," Jesse's new master, Vitus, responded. He brought his hand to Jesse's still throbbing, needy erection and gave his cock an idle stroke.

"And do you, Jesse, accept the absolute authority of the Lord Vitus over your mind, spirit, and body? Do you relinquish the right to disobey any command, and agree to comply instantly and with absolute loyalty and love, to his every whim? Do you swear to offer your body eagerly to Vitus and anyone else he commands? Do you promise to conduct his worldly affairs with diligence and good faith?"

Jesse raised his head and stared into the eyes of his master, his love. "I do."

"Then, according to the Dark Powers, I now pronounce you Vampire and Servant. My Lord, you may now use your thrall."

Jesse's cock surged. Throbbing between his legs, aching with need. Just twenty-four hours ago, he'd been Tom's bitch. Neglected emotionally, abused physically, and left wanting sexually. And now he had everything he wanted...almost.

The last twenty-four hours lacked only one thing: the sharp bite of pain. The impact of a hand or belt that woke the butterflies in his stomach and made him feel alive. The sting and subsequent burn that came from an angry strike sent a jolt of electricity to both Jesse's cock and animal brain. He didn't need it all the time, but when he did, he really needed it.

Vitus grabbed Jesse's chin and turned Jesse's face to meet his eyes. "I know," the vampire said. "I just vowed to meet all your needs. And since this is your first thought after becoming mine, I shall meet this one first, before you meet my needs, and the needs of all my friends."

Jesse's head spun. There were so many things to unpack there. Starting with: Vitus had read his mind. Read. His. Mind. And then, shit, and then servicing all his friends, a second night in a row? They'd have to call a doctor to stitch his asshole back to a regular size.

"Get over my knee," Vitus commanded.

Jesse obeyed, turning over on his handsome master's lap until his toes touched the floor on one side, his fingertips on the other, and his cock lay in the tight grip of the Lord Vampire's fabric clad legs.

The slapping blows of the vampire's hand were gentle at first, giving Jesse time to look around the room at the goings on. In front of him, both Onyx and Damien sat, wrapped in towels, at the feet of handsome, white-irised vampires on the closest couch. The crowd drew in, some standing with their hands on the backs of the sofas, others crouched beside the furniture, fangs bared, as if ready to strike. These put the fear into Jesse. And as the power and speed of Vitus's blows increased, the pain and fear traveled to Jesse's neglected cock. His shaft rubbed back and forth, chafing against the fabric of his master's pants.

"Don't you dare cum yet," Vitus admonished, sensing Jesse's thoughts.

The sting on Jesse's ass turned sharp. He cried out. The blows rattled him inside. It fucking *hurt*.

"Pain is one of the many ways my love enters your body," Vitus said. He punctuated this statement with a vicious strike to Jesse's ass. "Tell me you love me."

"I-ow! Fuck! I love you!"

Another strike.

"Again."

"I love you!" Jesse blurted quickly, before another heavy blow could interrupt him. His cock twitched with each strike, the lowest point on his body filling with blood, cum, and ever-increasing need. The heady, floating feeling traveled up his body to his brain, freeing him from all thought. He was only sensation now. Only need and fulfillment.

The blows rained down faster.

Around him, vampires and thralls shed their clothes.

The candles flickered.

"Up," Vitus commanded.

Jesse stood, his cock oozing long strings of pre-cum.

Vitus raised his arms and turned in a slow, wide circle as he said, "Now I believe it's traditional that we feast!"

The vampires cheered.

"Kai," Vitus gestured at the grate where Jesse had his shower.

Soda Can wheeled the suitcase containing Tom to the drain and unzipped it.

A pang shot through Jesse. He shouldn't care. And it embarrassed him that when he saw Tom's chest rise and fall, he felt relief.

Vitus turned to Jesse and frowned. Then turned back to the crowd. "Dinner is served!"

In a blur, the vampires around the room swarmed the suitcase. A circle of perfect, naked, vampires lifted Tom horizontally, holding him in the air.

"Bon appétit!" Vitus shouted.

As one, the vampires rose up, fangs exposed, then pounced on Tom. And Tom never opened his eyes.

It lasted only thirty seconds. And while the vampires feasted, and the blood flowed, Jesse turned to see Damien and Onyx making out, sitting on the floor by the empty chairs their masters had occupied only moments before.

Onyx waved him over.

Jesse didn't know if he should.

"It's all right," Damien assured him.

Jesse went to them, setting his bare, burning bottom on the cold concrete.

Onyx held his arms out. "Let me hold you while we watch our masters feast."

Jesse laid back into Onyx's arms, the beautiful man's hard cock pressed into the small of Jesse's back. Jesse tried not to notice. There was only one cock for him from now on.

One by one, the vampires left the feast, their cocks hard and swinging. They turned to the vampire closest and began kissing and stroking one another.

When Vitus did likewise, Jesse rose in a trance. He took in the view of the subterranean chamber. Glorious naked men of every description surrounded him. Big muscular hairy bears and smooth slender twinks stroked, fucked and sucked cocks of every description. Small, soft uncircumcised penises flopped back and forth under twinks, as hard muscled arms grabbed their hips and pounded thick meaty shafts into them. And in the center of it all, the last of the feasting vampires folded Tom's body back into the suitcase.

Moans bounced off the cement walls into Jesse's ears. Vitus, seated on his throne once again, caught Jesse's eye and pointed at his lap.

Jesse took the indicated seat on his master's thigh once again.

"Good boy," Vitus cooed, stroking Jesse's cheek. "Now for your reward."

Jesse's cock stood straight up between his naked thighs, untouched, throbbing with need.

"You did such a good job sucking and stroking all those cocks last night. Kneeling in the garbage and taking the cum offerings today. Such a good boy."

Jesse let out a low moan. His muscles stiffened. His cock

twitched and pulsed as if his master's words came out of the air and stroked him.

"Look into my eyes, Jesse."

Jesse did. The white irises showed a thousand sex acts so delicious and depraved that Jesse wanted to climb inside them, seeking release.

"Yes, yes, pet. You did such a good job. And I'm going to reward you. I'm going to give you just enough of my blood to strengthen you, fortify you against this cruel world. It is the utmost sign of both my love and ownership. And you are going to give me your orgasm. Your cum will show me, show all those present that you are my servant. My pet. My slave, and my mate, forever."

Jesse's mind closed in on itself. He tried to parse his master's words, but the pain in his bottom and the need in his cock refused to let his mind work.

Vitus raised his wrist to his lips. He bared his fangs and grazed his teeth along the skin. Blood dripped from his lord's wrist. The vampire held it to Jesse's lips. "Drink."

Jesse opened his mouth, accepting the vampire's cold flesh. The coppery taste of blood filled his mouth.

"Swallow," Vitus commanded.

Jesse did.

"Now," Vitus paused. He kissed Jesse's neck, scrapping stubble along the sensitive skin.

Shivers cascaded down Jesse's body. A powerful surge of energy gathered in his center. Building. Building.

"Now," Vitus repeated. "Cum." The vampire sank his fangs into Jesse's neck.

The pain and pleasure mixed. Taking blood and giving it. Giving love, and taking it. Taking it, and taking it. The ball of energy in his center slid along some secret sexual pathway inside him, traveling up his cock. Waves of intense pleasure crashed over Jesse like no other orgasm he'd ever experienced. His body quaked. His heart raced. The first jet of cum blasted out of his untouched cock. It sprayed under his chin, dripping down onto his chest as the next shot from inside him rained down on his thighs.

Still, he sucked, and still Vitus, his lord and master, sucked the crimson love from Jesse's neck. Another eruption pulsed from Jesse's cock. No one had touched his dick all day. Just Onyx's boot through the filthy fabric of his shorts. That this superior creature could make him cum with just a word, thrilled Jesse. The total submission and humiliation of the act drove Jesse to another plane of existence. Another shower of spunk jetted from his iron shaft. Jizz dripped down his balls, his chest, his thighs, his chin.

Over and over Jesse erupted cum, drenching himself and his master in an impossible amount of love milk. His orgasm seemed to last a lifetime, an eternity, an endless thunderstorm of lust. Even when there was no more fluid inside Jesse, his cock kept jerking in orgasm. And when he could take no more, Vitus released his neck and withdrew his wrist from Jesse's greedy, sucking mouth.

"Good boy," Vitus growled. "Stand."

Jesse tried to get to his feet, but wobbled helplessly.

Vitus caught his arm, steadying him. "Saxon, Pepper, hold him," Vitus commanded.

The world spun around Jesse, shaky and blurry. He'd cum so hard and lost so much blood, he wasn't sure he was even alive anymore. Instead, he felt as if he were some ghostly fuck animal, barely alive and that, only to serve the pleasure of his master.

Two vampires disentangled themselves from the tumult of gasping, sucking bodies around him, one black, the other white. Their cocks jutting ebony and ivory perfection, pointing at Jesse. They took his arms and held him on his trembling feet.

Vitus rose slowly from his chair. His thighs covered in milky droplets of Jesse's lust and submission. He approached slowly, not seeming to notice the dripping cum on his legs. His huge cock perfect and stiff as if carved from stone by a long dead Renaissance sculptor. "Turn him around."

The vampires holding Jesse traded arms and twisted him.

Fingers scooped jizz from Jesse's thighs and his chest, then roughly smeared the spend on his hole. The tip of his lord's cock bumped against Jesse's ass.

"Open for me," Vitus commanded.

And just like Jesse's orgasm, the simple order was enough to make it so. Jesse felt his ring open for his master's member, allowing it to slip easily inside him. He let out a gasp. A sigh of relief, as if being full of Vitus's cock was Jesse's natural state. As if without the lord vampire's dick inside him, Jesse wasn't complete. He had no meaning without a cock inside him, like a record with no player.

"Good pet," Vitus grunted.

The words stiffened Jesse's rod. It swung heavily between his legs as Vitus thrust his hips forward, impaling Jesse with his lord's love.

In front of Jesse, a beautiful blond twink mirrored him. Kai held the young man's arms. Long blond wavy hair spilled around the twink's face. And behind the bent over femboy, a large hairy vampire with pierced nipples pounded the smooth alabaster fem's hairless bottom.

"Kiss," Vitus commanded.

Onyx and Damien moved the twink closer.

Pepper and Saxon thrust Jesse forward as well until he stared in the eyes of blond waif. A mortal, like himself. The twink licked his lips.

Jesse pressed his face forward and tilted his head to the side.

Their lips met, soft skin pressed together. Wet tongues touched, then danced.

"Cum again!" Vitus grunted. His thrusts grew frenzied.

Jesse's cock bobbed between his legs. The irrepressible force burst from somewhere deep inside him, a ball of energy pumping from his lower chakra through his cock. Hot cum erupted from the angry head of Jesse's dick. The gooey rain spattered Jesse's stomach, then dripped to the floor.

"Fuck yes, you filthy little whore!" Vitus gave a mighty thrust, burying himself deep inside Jesse. Their balls met. Vitus's hot shaft pulsed and throbbed rhythmically in Jesse's hole.

Jesse moaned, accepting his master's spend. "Filling you with my love," Vitus grunted. "Take it like a good slut!"

Jesse's tongue danced with the mysterious blond twink. Their noses bumped as the big vampire bear behind blondie grunted and buried himself to the hilt into the smooth thin thrall.

Vitus slid his shaft out of Jesse.

Hot cum dribbled from Jesse's ruined hole and ran in sticky rivulets down his thigh. He felt so deliciously slutty and used. He'd never cum twice in a row so quickly. And he'd never cum without some kind of touch on his cock. Yet here tonight he'd had two mind bending orgasms without so much as the fingertip of his powerful vampire.

Vitus picked up the fluffy black towel from the chair and draped it over Jesse's shoulders. "Come," he had to whisper in Jesse's ear over the rising moans of the surrounding orgy. "Let me take you to my chamber, Love. It's time to start your new life."

ALSO BY CB CHELIAH

Look for the latest titles by CB Cheliah at freakyromance.com